This book should
Lancashire County

of the
shown

A H

10 APR 2017

bam 6/18

1 0 OCT 2019

THE BIG FELLOW

Young Inspector Jim Holland of Scotland Yard is under particular pressure to bring to justice 'The Big Fellow' — the mastermind behind a gang committing ever more audacious outrages. As the newspapers mount virulent attacks on Scotland Yard for failing to deal with the rogues, and the crimes escalate from robbery to brutal murder, Holland finds not only his own life threatened, but also that of his theatre actress girlfriend, Diana Carrington.

Also included is the story, *The Man on the Train*.

GERALD VERNER
and CHRIS VERNER

◆

THE BIG
FELLOW

Complete and Unabridged

LINFORD
Leicester

First published in Great Britain

First Linford Edition
published 2016

A catalogue record for this book is available
from the British Library.

ISBN 978–1–4448–3097–2

Published by
F. A. Thorpe (Publishing)
Anstey, Leicestershire

Set by Words & Graphics Ltd.
Anstey, Leicestershire
Printed and bound in Great Britain by
T. J. International Ltd., Padstow, Cornwall

This book is printed on acid-free paper

110052144

Contents

The Big Fellow

1

The Hold-Up

The spacious foyer of the Coronet Theatre was crowded. Crowds of soberly clad men and resplendent women laughed and chattered among themselves or passed from one to another exchanging greetings as they recognized friends and acquaintances among the fresh arrivals.

A seemingly never-ending stream of cars and taxi-cabs, their shining black roofs reflecting the glare from the overhead lamps, were constantly discharging their contents to add to the already dense throng that filled the vestibule.

It was the first night of a new comedy by an author whose name was world-famous, but even without that attraction, the name of Diana Carrington glittering in electric lights over the facia would have been sufficient to draw all play-loving London. A year ago she had been an unknown, obscure actress playing small parts in a provincial repertory company, had been seen by Shwartze, the producer, who, missing his train and having nothing better to do, had spent the evening at the local playhouse, and because she was just the type of fair-haired girl he wanted, he had engaged her there and then for the leading part in a production he was at that moment contemplating putting into rehearsal.

The girl's success had been phenomenal. She had awakened on the morning following the production of the play to find herself famous. Every newspaper rang with her name and although the play was a poor one and only ran for a month, the critics were unanimous in declaring that it owed even that modicum of success to Diana's clever acting. After that she had been inundated with offers from nearly every theatrical manager in London, but Shwartze had been clever and got her tied tip on a two-years' contract before the curtain fell on the last act.

The long line of vehicles before the

theatre was beginning to thin when a small grey coupé slowly nosed its way among the jam of traffic and was backed skilfully into a vacant place in the private car park opposite the entrance.

The young man who descended from the driving seat and pushed his way through the crowd might have been anything from twenty-two to thirty. In reality he was thirty-five, but his smooth boyish face and twinkling blue eyes gave him a false appearance of extreme youth. Detective Inspector James Holland, known throughout Scotland Yard from the Chief Commissioner down to the youngest constable as 'Jimmy,' had decided to take an evening off and enjoy himself — a rarity since the advent of 'The Big Fellow,' for that enterprising criminal had for the past eight months occupied his attention to the exclusion of all other matters.

How much his sudden decision to attend the first night of *Sheet Lightning* had been due to Diana Carrington's inclusion in the cast he was unwilling to admit even to himself. That it had to a considerable extent influenced him in choosing the Coronet as a place of entertainment he couldn't deny, but why it should have done so was a question he preferred to leave unanswered — for the present.

Hurrying up the steps to the rapidly emptying vestibule, for the curtain was timed to rise at eight, and it wanted but a few minutes to the hour, Jim paused and looked about him.

Two men who had been standing talking by the box-office saw him and came forward. The elder, a tall, red-faced man with greying hair and a humorous gleam in his deep-set eyes, extended a hand in greeting.

'You're late,' he remarked in a pleasant voice. 'We'd almost given you up.'

Jim smiled an apology as he shook hands.

'From a most prosaic cause,' he replied. 'I lost my collar stud.'

'What did you do?' inquired the other's companion. 'Send for the Flying Squad?'

'Much as it may surprise you, Harry,' said Jim gravely, 'I succeeded in finding it all by myself.'

Harry Littleton, crime reporter on the *Megaphone*, chuckled, his fat face creasing with innumerable wrinkles.

'The training of a detective has its uses, after all,' he said. 'Now when *I* lose a stud I can never find the damned thing.'

'A person of your build is not expected to,' retorted Jim. 'Being a reporter, you would merely send for the police and then write up two columns of lurid sensationalism, concluding with some scathing remarks about the incompetency of Scotland Yard.'

'That's one up to you, Jim,' laughed the grey-haired man, and then, as a burst of music sounded from inside: 'Come on, the overture's started — we might as well go in.'

He led the way up a flight of carpeted stairs, where an attendant met them, took the ticket Jim held out, and conducted them along a corridor, stopping outside a rosewood door. Jim Holland had been lucky in securing a box, for the theatre was booked out weeks before the premiere and he had only made up his mind to go that afternoon. It was only because the people who had originally taken the box were prevented from coming at the last moment that Jim had managed to get it. Unwilling to go alone, he had telephoned Harry Littleton and Leslie Venning and, finding that they had nothing particular to do that evening, had persuaded them to join him.

The theatre was rapidly filling as they took their seats, though there still remained blocks of empty stalls here and there awaiting the inevitable latecomers who seem to find it impossible to get to a theatre until halfway through the first act, to the inconvenience and annoyance of the people they have to disturb to reach their seats.

'How did you manage to tear yourself away from work, Jim?' asked Venning, settling himself in his chair and lighting a cigar, for being commercially minded the management of the Coronet allowed smoking. 'Every time I've tried to get at you lately, you've put me off with the excuse of being too busy.'

'I am still,' answered Jim. 'But an hour or two won't make any difference and even a detective must have a little amusement.'

'Any further news about 'The Big Fellow'?' asked Harry. It was the *Megaphone* that had first given him that name.

Jim shook his head.

'Nothing,' he replied.

'He's been very quiet lately, hasn't he?' mused Venning, examining the end of his cigar.

'Too quiet.' Jim's brows wrinkled in a frown. 'It's a fortnight since he raided Shottard's in Bond Street and got away with close on £100,000 worth of jewellery — in broad daylight too.'

'I wonder if you fellows'll ever catch him,' said Harry, crossing his legs and tilting his chair at a more comfortable angle. 'He must be jolly clever or he wouldn't have evaded capture for so long.'

'He *is* clever,' answered Jim. 'But I'll get him in the end. The people who work for him don't count' — he snapped his fingers — 'not that. We pulled in two of them over the Moss Bank affair. They're just ordinary little crooks, not a brain among them, and without their leader they'd be done. It's he who makes them dangerous.'

'You're no nearer discovering who *he* is, I suppose?' said Venning.

Jim shrugged his shoulders. 'Not more than we were eight months ago,' he answered wearily. 'He's just a name and a brain, and nothing more. Even the members of his own gang have never seen him, if we can believe the story those two fellows tell. By the way, you're defending them, aren't you?'

Leslie Venning, one of the cleverest K.C.'s of the day, nodded slowly.

'Who retained you?' asked Jim curiously. 'I've been going to ask you ever since I heard about it.'

'Sellers, of Sellers and Ruler,' answered Venning. 'They are quite well-known solicitors and thoroughly respectable.'

'But they must have received instructions from someone,' persisted Jim.

'They did.' Venning blew out a cloud of smoke. 'The money for all fees and typewritten instructions to retain my services were received by letter on the morning following that on which Crean and Lewston were committed for trial. Needless to say, the letter bore neither signature nor address.'

Harry Littleton passed his hand carefully over the top of his shining fair hair.

'It came from 'The Big Fellow', of course,' he said.

'Of course,' agreed Jim thoughtfully. 'You know that I've been given *carte blanche* to 'cover' this business,' Harry continued. 'Old 'Baldy'' — the news-editor of the *Megaphone* thus irreverently referred to was without hair on his head — 'would give his soul for an exclusive story about them. So don't forget to let me know if you get a line on 'The Big Fellow'.'

'You'll know,' answered Jim grimly and turned his attention to the auditorium.

The house was crowded and the multi-hued dresses of the women showed up in relief against the conventional black and white of the men's attire. The soft lights struck sparks of living fire from the jewels gleaming against creamy throats and arms, the whole presenting a kaleidoscopic picture of vivid colour.

With a final blare of brass and drums, the orchestra died to silence, the lights dimmed and the curtain rose on the first act.

It was a very ordinary comedy, relying for its laughs more on broad humour than witty dialogue, but for all Jim knew about it, it might have been a masterpiece. He had eyes for no one except the tall, graceful girl who, from her first entrance, bore the greater part of the play on her slim shoulders.

He forgot crime, forgot for the moment that there was even such a place as Scotland Yard, while he watched, fascinated, her every movement and listened to the sweet, musical cadence of a voice that was never raised yet was audible in every corner of the building.

Jim Holland had first met Diana two months ago and the method of his meeting had not lacked excitement. A bag-snatcher had made a grab at the girl's handbag while she was walking along a quiet street on her way home after the theatre and Jim had happened to be near at hand. The sneak-thief made off at his approach, but had succeeded in getting away with the bag, which contained all her money. Diana lived in a block of flats at Victoria and Jim had insisted on sending her home in a taxi, for the episode had shaken her nerves.

He met her again by accident in a teashop, two days after, raised his hat and was recognized. It had been the beginning of many meetings and they had drifted into a friendship. Twice he had taken her out to dinner and discovered that she was companionable as well as pretty — a rare trait. His real feeling for her he refused to allow himself to analyse, although more than once he had found himself counting the hours to the time when he could reasonably make an excuse to see her again.

The curtain fell on the first act amidst a thunder of applause, rose and fell again. As it descended for the last time, Venning got up and stretched himself.

'Come and have a drink,' he suggested; a suggestion that was eagerly seconded by Harry, who had sat throughout the act with a somewhat bored expression on his round, good-natured face.

As they made their way towards the buffet, Jim suddenly caught sight of a familiar face among the crowd. With a muttered apology to his companions, he slipped after the big, stout man in evening dress who had attracted his attention. He swung round as Jim touched him on the shoulder and his rather florid face went a shade paler.

'Good evening, 'Tiny'!' said Holland genially. 'Enjoying the show?'

The other recovered himself and raised his eyebrows at the familiarity.

'I'm afraid you've made a mistake — ' he began, but something in Jim's face stopped him.

'No.' Jim shook his head sadly. 'It won't do — it really won't do.'

'What won't do?'

'It's no use pretending. I never make mistakes.' He took the stout man affectionately by the arm. 'Poor 'Tiny'! It's really too bad!'

The fat man sighed heavily.

'See here, Mr. Holland, I'm not doing

anything against the law,' he said in an injured voice. 'Surely a fellow can enjoy himself without being interfered with by you 'busys'!'

Jim chuckled softly.

'Surely,' he agreed, 'it all depends upon how you intend to enjoy yourself. It worries me to see a clever crook like you having temptation put in his way.'

He glanced at the crowd of bejewelled women moving around them. The other followed the direction of his eyes and shook his head.

'You're wrong, Mr. Holland,' he said. 'I'm running straight — I am really.'

'Tell me another,' suggested Jim.

'It's a fact,' affirmed his companion. 'At least' — he paused cautiously — 'I'm not here on business tonight.'

'What are you here for, then?' inquired Jim. 'You're not going to make me believe you've suddenly become a lover of the drama.'

'No.' The man addressed as 'Tiny' shook his head. 'I'm here out of curiosity.'

Jim looked at him in astonishment. He was quite serious.

'I want to see what's going to happen,' he continued softly. 'Something's going to happen, and I want to know what.'

'What do you mean?'

'Tiny' drew a long breath and looked about him.

'I don't know,' he muttered, 'and if I did, I shouldn't tell you. But I've heard things.'

'What things?' asked Jim sharply.

'Just rumours,' answered the other evasively. 'I can't tell you any more, Mr. Holland, honestly I can't, because I don't know.'

Jim tried his best to get the man to say more, but he either wouldn't or couldn't, and eventually he returned to his box with a vague feeling of disquiet.

The second act had started as he entered softly, but the stage no longer held his attention. His mind was groping to try and find an explanation for 'Tiny's' presence and his cryptic remarks.

Sam Plant, known as 'Tiny' on account of his immense size, was one of the cleverest jewel thieves in London and he was far too clever to risk a chance haul.

What was it then he expected to happen?

And then suddenly, while Jim was still thinking, every light on the stage went out and the theatre was plunged in darkness!

An excited murmur broke out from the audience.

'What the devil's happened?' Jim heard Harry's question from the darkness close at hand, but before he could reply a loud, harsh voice rose above the noise below. It came from the darkness of the stage.

'If everyone will remain in their seats, they will be unharmed.'

There was a second's dead silence and then, as suddenly as they had gone out, the lights came on again.

'Good God!' breathed Jim, and leaned forward over the edge of the box.

At every exit stood a man in evening dress, his face concealed by a rubber gas mask, his right hand holding aloft a glass bomb!

'Tiny' Plant's curiosity had been satisfied!

2

The Get-Away

For a moment a deathly stillness reigned over the whole building, broken at length by a woman's hysterical scream. It was followed by a general movement that was checked by the voice that had spoken before. It came from a man who stood upon the stage, his back to the safety curtain, which, during the short interval of darkness, had been lowered. He also was in evening dress, but the mask he wore had been raised sufficiently to enable him to use a small megaphone, though not enough to be able to see his face.

'Let no one move!' The tone was authoritative and every word slow and distinct. 'Each glass bomb held by the men at the exits contains a highly concentrated form of poison gas. The breaking of all bombs would release enough vapour to kill every living soul in this building. We are taking no chances and the slightest attempt to move from your seats will result in the breaking of the bombs!'

As the harsh, metallic voice of the speaker ceased, Jim made an involuntary movement to rise.

'Sit down!' A muffled voice behind him caused the young inspector to turn. The door of the box was open and on the threshold stood a man exactly similar to those stationed at the exits. The eyepieces of his mask glinted in the light and gave him a curiously weird appearance. 'You are quite safe as long as you remain quiet,' came the warning. 'Otherwise — ' He made a gesture with the glass globe he held in his hand and the threat was unmistakable.

'You can't do anything, Jim,' muttered Harry quickly, 'except keep still. It would be madness to resist. They've got us in the hollow of their hands.'

Realizing his utter helplessness, Jim relapsed into his seat with a shrug of his shoulders.

The man on the stage had begun speaking again and he turned his attention to the auditorium.

'The instructions I am about to give to you, you will follow to the letter,' came the order. 'I have already told you the result if any of you attempt to disobey.' He paused for a second and then continued. 'Beginning with Row A. of the stalls, you will empty your pockets, take off all jewellery and pass it to the person sitting next you, who will repeat the operation and hand the whole to the person next to them and so on until it reaches the man waiting at the end of the row to receive it. Row B. will do the same and each row following suit up to the last row, as also will those occupying the dress circle. Is that clear? Start!'

He finished amidst a breathless hush and then a rustle of sound filled the theatre as the instructions he had given were carried out. Men began to empty their pockets, women to take off their jewels, and the pile of notes, wallets and jewellery grew to huge proportions as it passed from hand to hand down each row and was received in a sack held by the masked man waiting at the end for that purpose. It was curiously reminiscent of a hospital collection he had seen, Jim thought, as he watched spellbound. The sheer audacity of the raid took his breath away and he couldn't help feeling a tinge of admiration for the brain that had planned this colossal coup.

In an incredibly short space of time, six bulging sacks had been filled and these were carried out through the swing exit doors. The man on the stage waited until the last had disappeared, then he drew out his watch and glanced at it. Two minutes dragged slowly by — two minutes that seemed to Jim an age — then suddenly the man raised his megaphone.

'Right!' he roared, and the word had scarcely left his lips when the theatre was again plunged in complete darkness.

For nearly half a minute there was silence, a silence so intense that it could almost be felt, and then pandemonium broke out. Men shouted, women screamed. There was a clatter of raising seats as the nerves of the overstrained audience broke.

Jim rose quickly to his feet and, groping his way to the door, cannoned into someone who was making for the same objective.

'Unless somebody can get the lights on again, there'll be a panic,' said the voice of Venning at his elbow.

Jim felt in his pocket and found the box of matches he was seeking and the next moment a feeble glimmer illumined the darkness. The door of the box was open, but the masked man who had been on guard had disappeared.

Followed by Harry and Venning, Jim made his way down the corridor, striking matches to guide him. The emergency gas lamps insisted upon by the L.C.C. rules in all public buildings were out and must have been turned off from the main — another proof of the careful way in which the hold-up had been planned.

They reached the stairs as Holland's last match gave out and had to feel their way down by the brass rail.

The noise in the theatre was becoming

deafening. As they reached the swing doors giving on to the stalls, the lights went up. Someone apparently who had still retained their presence of mind had found the main switch. Jim saw a congested crowd of scared-looking men and white-faced, half-fainting women, and turned to his companions.

'If we go in there we shall never get out,' he said, and turned on down the corridor towards the foyer. It was brilliantly lighted, but deserted, and Jim learned afterwards that the outside lights in the vestibule and front of the theatre had never gone out.

He went over to the box office. It was empty, but the door at the side was open and, looking in, he saw the figure of the clerk in charge doubled up on the floor. He was still breathing, and a quick glance told Jim that the man had been drugged. He turned to the telephone and lifted the receiver, but there was no answering call from the exchange — the line had been cut somewhere.

'Thorough,' was his mental comment, as he set the useless instrument down.

He caught sight of a uniformed policeman passing the front as he came out of the office and sent Harry after him.

The constable listened in growing amazement when Holland briefly told him what had happened.

'It beats anything I've ever 'eard,' he gasped, scratching his chin.

'Or anything you're ever likely to,' snapped Jim, and sent the bewildered policeman to telephone a message to headquarters.

Venning's voice calling him took Jim over to where the K.C. was bending down by a screen of palms and flowers.

'Look here!' he said, and pointed.

Hidden by the foliage was the body of a burly commissionaire. A brief examination showed that he had been treated in the same way as the ticket clerk.

Jim shrugged his shoulders in despair and, leaving Venning and Harry in the foyer, went back inside the theatre in search of the manager.

He saw him, a stout, dishevelled man in evening dress, standing by the orchestra rail, trying to quiet the restive audience and hoarse with his efforts to make himself heard above the noise.

Waiting until he had finished his speech, Jim forced his way through the throng to his side.

The manager turned a streaming face towards him as he made known his identity.

'This is a dreadful business, Mr. Holland,' he panted, 'terrible!'

'It might have been worse,' said Jim unsympathetically. 'Listen — no one is to leave this building until my men arrive. You'd better tell 'em.'

'I'll do my best,' said the greatly worried man, and turned to address the crowd once more.

Jim left his side and was making his way back to the exit when somebody touched his arm. He looked down. 'Tiny' Plant was by his elbow.

'Well,' he asked softly, 'what did you think of it?'

'I'll tell you presently,' replied Jim. 'I shall want to hear quite a lot from you.'

Sam Plant looked pained.

'I know nothing about it,' he protested.

'You surely don't think it had anything to do with me, do you? Why, it nearly broke my heart to see all that good stuff goin' into those sacks. They took a watch and a gold cigarette case of mine too. Both honestly paid for,' he added sadly.

'Too bad!' said Jim. 'You knew this was going to happen and I want to know how you knew.'

The jewel thief shook his head.

'I can't tell you that,' he answered. 'I would if I could, but I — daren't! It 'ud be as much as my life was worth.'

'It'll be as much as your liberty's worth if you don't,' snapped Jim shortly.

'You've nothing on me, Mr. Holland,' said Plant quickly. 'Nothing at all, and you can't make me talk.'

'We'll see about that,' retorted Holland, and hurried off to the vestibule.

Arrived there, he found that his message to the 'Yard' had taken effect.

Four police tenders were drawn up outside the theatre and the foyer was full of plainclothes men. Detective Sergeant Wiles, a tall, thin, melancholy man, approached Jim as he made his appearance.

'I've thrown a cordon round the building, sir,' he said, 'according to your instructions. 'The Big Fellow' again, ain't it?'

Jim nodded and told him what had happened.

'Clever,' he remarked, when the young inspector finished. 'And original. Don't think I've heard of a hold-up in a theatre before. Banks and shops, but not a theatre. There must have been a lot of them to work it.'

'Nearly thirty men, I should think,' said Jim.

'As many as that?' The sergeant seemed surprised. 'I wonder who the fellow was who did the talking? 'The Big Fellow' himself, I suppose?'

Jim shook his head.

'No, I don't think so,' he replied. 'He's never taken an active part before.'

'Humph!' Wiles ruminated. 'I wonder — '

What it was he wondered Jim wasn't destined to know, for at that moment a uniformed sergeant came up and reported that the cloakroom attendants had been found unconscious in an anteroom and Wiles turned away to issue instructions

The audience began trickling out into the vestibule and, marshalled by several officers of the Flying Squad, were formed into a line that had to pass a sergeant who took particulars of each person before they were allowed to leave.

Jim watched this dreary routine work for some time and was still watching when Leslie Venning came up to say good night.

'Let me know if you discover anything fresh,' he said as he shook hands.

'I'll ring you up in the morning,' promised Jim, and beckoned one of his men. 'Take Mr. Venning through the cordon,' he ordered. 'You'll never get out otherwise,' he added with a smile.

A doctor who had been among the audience was in attendance on the unconscious staff. The box office clerk and the commissionaire had already recovered and their stories were practically identical. A man in evening dress, presumably a member of the audience, had come out during the second act with a handkerchief pressed over his nose and mouth. He had complained of feeling ill and called the commissionaire. When the man came up, something had been sprayed in his face and he lost consciousness. The remainder of the staff, it was afterwards discovered, had suffered a similar experience. None of them was able to say with certainty what the men were like or thought they would be able to recognize them again. In each case the handkerchief had been used to conceal the face.

An inquiry at the back revealed the fact that the stage-door keeper had been treated in a like manner. A man in a heavy coat with a muffler over his chin had come in the stage-door and before the keeper had time to inquire his business, the spray had been used and he remembered no more.

'I was standing at the back of the circle,' said the flustered manager to Jim, 'when the lights went out. I thought at first that something had gone wrong at the power station. It all seems to me like a nightmare. What the directors'll say I don't know.'

Jim wasn't particularly interested in what the directors would say and intimated the fact plainly. Sergeant Wiles came up and reported that a pile of gas masks and gas bombs had been found in the circle and stalls bars.

'It's pretty easy to see how they made their get-away,' he said lugubriously. 'When the lights went out the second time, they had only to take off the masks, get rid of the bombs and mingle again with the audience. Clever but simple — all clever things are simple.'

'You must be very clever,' said Harry Littleton, an interested listener.

Wiles looked at him suspiciously, but the reporter's face was mask-like, and he turned again to Jim.

'They got the stuff away in a closed car. Several people saw it drive away.'

'Number?' asked Jim laconically.

Wiles shook his head.

'Nobody knows,' he replied bitterly. 'There was a whole string of cars outside. It was only one among many — that's a quotation from something or other, isn't it? It wouldn't have been noticed at all only they saw the sacks being put in. Thought they were something to do with the theatre. Well?' This to the sergeant who had been taking the names and addresses of the audience.

'That's the lot.' The sergeant closed a bulky notebook with a snap.

Wiles took it and dropped it into the side pocket of his overcoat.

'All right,' he said. 'I don't suppose it's going to help us much, but you never can tell. Most of the gang must have been among that lot, but I expect they've given false names, and if they haven't, we've no means of finding out who they were.'

'We've detained Sam Plant, sir,' said the sergeant to Jim. 'Perhaps you'd like to see him.'

Jim nodded slowly.

'Lead us to him,' he said and, accompanied by Wiles, followed the sergeant up the stairs.

They found 'Tiny' Plant pacing up and down the cloakroom, guarded by a plainclothes man, and for an hour they questioned him, but without result. The only thing they could get him to say was that he had heard rumours that something was to happen at the Coronet that night, but where or from whom he heard it, he absolutely refused to divulge. Wiles gave it up at length in despair.

'It's impossible to make him talk,' he whispered to Jim. 'Of course we can detain him as a suspect and try again tomorrow.'

Jim shook his head.

'No, don't do that,' he said. 'Let him go and get a man to watch him. We're more likely to learn something that way.'

The hour was getting late and there was very little more that could be done, and Jim, who was almost dropping with weariness, was considering going home when he suddenly remembered the girl and decided to call round at the back and see her. He found Harry Littleton outside as he descended the steps of the entrance, on the point of hurrying off to the *Megaphone* offices to turn in an account of the affair.

The news of the raid had leaked out

and the pavement was crowded with a collection of staring sightseers clustered together in little whispering groups.

Jim saw Harry off in a taxi and then made his way round to the stage-door.

The officer on duty there saluted as the young inspector appeared.

'Miss Carrington?' he repeated in answer to Jim's inquiry. 'I think she's gone, sir. I'll just make sure.'

He called to another man further down the passage and put the question.

'The young lady left about an hour ago,' was the reply. 'She wasn't feeling well and as there was nothing to detain her for, Sergeant Wiles took her address and told her she could go home.'

Jim Holland felt disappointed, but not surprised. Several hours had elapsed since the hold-up and he had hardly expected to find the girl still there. He made up his mind to call round and see her some time during the following morning.

He remained talking to the man in charge for some time and learned that the procedure at the back had been identical with that in the front of the house.

Having disposed of the stage-door keeper, ten men had taken possession of the stage and the electric switchboard from which all the lights in the place were controlled. In face of the gas bombs they carried, it had been impossible to resist.

'It was a daring thing to do,' said the Scotland Yard man admiringly, 'but they got away with it. The organization was wonderful. This 'Big Fellow', or whatever he calls himself, has got brains. He thinks of everything.'

'There's one thing he hasn't thought of,' said Jim, as he turned to leave.

'What's that, sir?' asked the man interestedly.

'That no human being is infallible. The cleverest man is bound sooner or later to make a mistake and our mysterious friend isn't an exception although his colossal vanity probably makes him think he is. He'll make that mistake one day and when he does, we've got him.'

He went on to find Wiles and say good night. That lugubrious official, looking more depressed than ever, was standing on the steps of the main entrance, staring at the pavement.

He glanced up at Jim and shook his head sadly when the young inspector wished him good night.

'It's not a 'good' night, Mr. Holland,' he said, 'and it's not going to be a 'good' morning either. The 'heads' are going to be rattled over this. There's bound to be an inquiry. We shall be hauled up on the mat for this little party.'

Jim clapped him on the shoulder.

'For heaven's sake, cheer up!' he smiled. 'They may have us on the mat, but they can't tread on us. After all, it's not our fault.'

'People are so unreasonable.' Wiles scratched his chin dolefully. 'Some of 'em 'ud blame the police if it was a wet day.'

Jim left him still staring at the pavement and went in search of his car. He lived in a little flat in a quiet thoroughfare off Oxford Street and because his heart ached and his eyes felt hot and prickly, he left the car at his garage in Wardour Street and decided to walk the short distance home. It was that hour when London is at its quietest, when the street-cleaners are out swilling down the roads, and the air was sweet and cool to his throbbing temples.

Swinging out of Wardour Street, Jim was in the act of crossing the road when he saw two people, a man and a girl, coming towards him engaged in earnest conversation. Something in the girl's appearance attracted his attention. It seemed familiar. He drew back into the shadow of a shop doorway and waited for them to pass. They came on slowly and as they drew almost level with him, the light from a street standard fell full upon their faces. Jim choked back the startled exclamation that rose to his lips. For the girl was Diana Carrington and the man she was talking to so earnestly was the fat jewel thief, 'Tiny' Plant!

3

The Photograph

It seemed to Jim Holland that he had been asleep for about ten minutes when Punt, his servant, woke him with a cup of tea. Struggling up on one elbow, he blinked himself to wakefulness and glanced at the clock on the table by his bedside. The hands pointed to half-past eight. The hot tea roused him a little, but he still felt terribly tired and it needed a strong effort to prevent himself from turning over and going to sleep again. He succeeded in mastering the almost overpowering inclination, and dragging himself out of bed, slipped on a dressing-gown and made his way to the bathroom. A cold bath and a shower had the effect of almost restoring him to normal, and by the time he had shaved and was sitting down to the appetizing breakfast that Punt had prepared, all desire for further slumber had left him. He still felt tired, but it was more weariness of spirit than bodily fatigue.

The events of the preceding night came crowding thick and fast into his brain and foremost among them was his chance discovery of the intimacy that apparently existed between Diana and Sam Plant. The more he thought about it, the more puzzled he became. What could a girl like Diana have in common with a man of 'Tiny's' character — a known jewel thief who had served more than one sentence and whose record took up a considerable space in a certain room at Scotland Yard reserved for the particulars of such people?

He pondered over the matter all through his breakfast, but reached no satisfactory conclusion except a determination to question Diana about it at the first opportunity.

Having reached this decision and also the end of his meal, Jim turned his attention to the morning papers. They 'splashed' the latest exploit of 'The Big Fellow' in flaming headlines across the front page, but it was only the *Megaphone* that gave any very clear account of what had actually happened, and Harry's effort was masterly in its graphic description of what he styled the 'sensation of the century.'

Jim chuckled as he read, but the smile faded from his lips when he caught sight of the leader page and the article it contained.

It was a virulent attack upon the methods of the police and a demand for an inquiry concerning what it termed 'the apparent hopeless incompetence of Scotland Yard to deal with this dangerous gang who are a menace to the lives and property of the people. Now is the time,' the article concluded, 'for the Home Secretary to prove that he is the right man in the right place. It is over eight months since the organization first came into existence and nothing has been done to check their nefarious progress. Let Sir Robert Mallet take the matter in hand, and if necessary insist upon the institution of new blood at headquarters. It is badly wanted.'

The rest of the papers were all in the same strain, though not quite so vitriolic as the *Megaphone,* and Jim set off for the Yard with a feeling of acute depression.

The message that awaited him from the Assistant Commissioner on his arrival at his office did nothing to dissipate this feeling, for it was terse and to the point. Jim walked down the long corridor towards the great man's room with a heavy heart.

'Come in, Holland,' said Colonel Allen, looking up from behind a big table littered with papers when he tapped and entered. 'I suppose you've seen the papers this morning?'

Jim assented and sat down on the other side of the desk.

'Something will have to be done,' went on the Assistant Commissioner gravely, helping himself to a cigarette. 'You've been in charge of this matter for over seven months and up to the present you've failed.'

'I've done my best, sir,' said Jim.

'I'm not saying you haven't.' The

Colonel blew a cloud of smoke ceiling-ward. 'I consider you a very capable officer and I realize your difficulties. But you've fallen down badly on this case and as I say something has got to be done — and done soon.'

'I hope to be able to supply some definite information in the course of the next few days,' said Jim. 'Don't think I'm trying to excuse myself. I'm not — I'm stating a fact. If we can find the man who runs the outfit the others don't matter, they'd go to pieces without him.'

The Assistant Commissioner removed his cigarette from his lips before speaking.

'Why do you say '*him*'?' he asked slowly. 'What makes you so certain that it is a *man*?'

Jim Holland was so surprised that for a moment he was incapable of speech.

'I don't quite understand, sir,' he stammered.

'There is no evidence to show that 'The Big Fellow' isn't a woman!' The Colonel leaned slightly forward as he spoke. 'It's only a suggestion of mine. Think it over!'

He nodded a dismissal and Jim

returned to his own office, his mind in a whirl. The interview had not been as bad as he had anticipated, but the Assistant Commissioner's concluding remarks had given him a considerable amount to think about.

Sergeant Wiles was waiting for him and his greeting was sympathetic.

'Had a bad time?' he asked, and when Jim replied in the negative: 'I'm glad. Thought you would have. You've seen the papers, of course — pleasant little fellows! The reports have come in about last night's hold-up.'

'Anything fresh?' Jim forced his mind to take an interest in what the sergeant was saying.

Wiles shook his head.

'No. Did you expect anything?' he replied dubiously.

'I didn't. 'Tiny' Plant gave the man who was trailing him the slip at Piccadilly Circus. I've given him a rowing — not Plant, the fellow who was following him, I mean. Are you listening?'

The reference to Sam Plant had switched Jim's thoughts back to the incident in Oxford Street and subconsciously he coupled it with the Assistant Commissioner's astounding suggestion. Could Colonel Allen have been referring to Diana when —

'It's impossible!' Jim made the remark aloud, and Sergeant Wiles regarded him curiously.

'I don't know what you're talking about,' he said, 'but I quite agree with you it's all impossible. There was a fellow once who said that nothing was impossible, wasn't there? He'd never heard of 'The Big Fellow'.'

He sighed.

'He's the most impossible thing that ever happened, and the more you think of him, the more impossible he becomes. 1 like that word impossible — it kind of fits the situation. There's another word that would do just as well, but I can't think of it.'

Jim let him ramble on. In spite of his peculiarities he knew that Wiles was one of the cleverest officers in the C.I.D. and he had chosen him as his assistant above all others when he had first been put in charge of the case.

The sergeant took his departure soon after to follow up an inquiry concerning the car in which the sacks of jewellery had been taken away, and, as soon as he was left alone, Jim drew the telephone towards him and gave a Victoria number.

In a few minutes he was connected and presently heard the low, sweet voice of Diana from the other end of the wire.

'Who is that?'

'Jim — Jim Holland,' he replied, and his heart beat a trifle faster at the sound of her voice. 'I thought I'd ring up and see how you were after last night.'

'Wasn't it dreadful?' He thought her voice trembled slightly, but put it down to imagination. 'I was terribly frightened. I don't think 1 shall feel really happy in the theatre again.'

'Are you playing tonight?' he asked.

'Oh, yes! Mr. Shwartze says that the show couldn't have had any better advertisement.'

'There are a lot of people who won't agree with Mr. Shwartze,' said Jim a trifle grimly. 'What are you doing this afternoon? Would you care to meet me for tea somewhere?'

'I should love to, but I've already promised to have tea with a friend.' She hesitated. 'I'm free at lunch-time tomorrow.'

'All right then. I'll meet you at the Carltonian at one o'clock.' He scribbled the appointment on his blotting pad. 'I came round last night to see you, but you'd gone.'

'Did you? That was kind of you. I got away as soon as I could and went home. I was feeling terribly upset.'

'Did you go straight home?' inquired Jim.

'Of course.' She sounded surprised. 'Why did you ask that?'

'I — I thought I saw you — in — in Oxford Street,' he stammered. 'About — three — '

'It couldn't have been me.' She laughed. 'I was in bed and asleep. You made a mistake. Goodbye till tomorrow!'

There was a click as she hung up the receiver and Jim pushed the telephone away from him with a sudden feeling of sickness.

She had been lying and the knowledge hurt him. That it was she he had seen talking to Sam Plant he was certain. And the fact that she had lied proved that there was something she wished to conceal.

With a weary sigh, Jim stretched out his hand and pressed a bell on his desk.

To the constable who answered his summons he gave an order.

'Go along to records, Smithson, and ask them to let me have all the information they've got concerning important women criminals at present at liberty. I don't want the little shoplifters — I want the big crooks.'

The constable saluted and hurried away. Jim rose to his feet and strolled over to the window, gazing out moodily on the rain-swept embankment. He remained there for some time, lost in thought, until he was aroused from his reverie by the return of the policeman, his arms full of bulky folders. He laid them down on Jim's desk, and when he had withdrawn, the young inspector settled himself down to work.

Hour after hour went by while he read through the voluminous records containing items of information regarding every known female criminal.

He put aside those whom he thought were capable of controlling an organization like the 'Big Fellow's' and they were few. It was late in the afternoon when he opened the last folder and the first thing he saw caused him to sit suddenly bolt upright. On the top of the pile was a photograph and underneath on an official blank the description relating to it.

'Florence Drew,' read Jim. 'Six months' imprisonment with hard labour for larceny. Holloway Prison. Released June 8th, 1926. Five previous convictions.' There followed a long description and then in red ink: 'This woman is dangerous.'

'Good God!' breathed Jim, for the face in the photograph was the face of Diana Carrington!

4

The Soup

Diana Carrington dressed with care. She was a tall slim girl, who looked twenty but was in reality six years older. The success that had come to her had left her unspoiled in that she was completely unaffected.

She looked at herself in the mirror over her dressing-table, passed a powder-puff swiftly over her face, touched her lips with scarlet and nodded with satisfaction. She was picking up her gloves when the postman came, and a moment later her maid entered with a letter.

Diana took the envelope and at the sight of the handwriting her face whitened. She looked so ill that the maid was alarmed.

'What's the matter, miss?' she asked anxiously.

48

'Nothing.' Diana found a chair and sat down. 'I felt a little giddy, that's all.'

'Would you like me to get you anything?' The maid eyed her doubtfully.

She shook her head.

'No, no, I shall be all right directly.' And then, as the woman turned away: 'You might phone for a taxi, please.'

She waited until she was alone and then, with trembling fingers, she ripped open the flap of the envelope and extracted the contents.

The letter was a short one covering half one side of a single sheet of paper, and as she read a look of despair crossed her face.

She read the note twice and then, in her hand, she sat staring unseeingly in front of her, pale to the lips.

A grisly ghost had arisen in her life — a ghost that she had hoped was laid for good.

Her maid announcing the arrival of the taxi roused her, and, thrusting the crumpled letter into her bag, she took a last glance at herself in the mirror and hurried downstairs to the cab.

Jim was waiting in the lounge when she arrived at the Carltonian and greeted her with unconcealed pleasure. She noted the dark circles under his eyes and the lines about his mouth, eloquent testimony of the strain through which he was living.

He led her into the big grill-room and the head waiter came forward and found them a table by the window.

Jim watched the girl as she stripped off her gloves, and wondered. It seemed impossible that the dainty figure before him could ever have been a criminal. And yet the photograph was irrefutable evidence. The girl was known to the police, and however incredible it appeared, had been labelled a dangerous woman.

Jim sighed involuntarily.

Diana looked up from a refractory button and met his eyes.

'What's the matter?' she asked. 'You sound depressed.'

'I am, rather,' he admitted, picking up the menu.

'Why?' And then, as he made no reply: 'Is it the affair at the theatre that's worrying you?'

'Partly.' He tried hard to prevent himself becoming monosyllabic, but failed.

'It was a dreadful affair, wasn't it?' She leaned back, one slim hand resting on the table. 'I suppose you haven't found out who the people were who were responsible?'

Jim shook his head.

'Beyond knowing it was the work of 'The Big Fellow', no,' he answered.

'Haven't you any idea who he is?' she asked.

'Not the slightest,' he replied. 'I'd give a lot to find out.'

He paused as a waiter came up to take their order and was silent until after the man had gone. Then he continued:

'This 'Big Fellow' is the brain behind it all. The motive force. Destroy that and the rest automatically destroys itself.'

'And don't you know who he is?' she inquired again. 'Haven't you any clue to his identity?'

'No. Sometimes I begin to wonder if we ever shall.'

She lapsed into silence and Jim,

noticing her preoccupation, wondered what it was that had suddenly made her so thoughtful.

This girl with the flawless face and soft voice, whom he had met but half a dozen times in his life, meant more to him than he cared to admit. There must be some explanation for that photograph in the record department other than appeared on the surface. Knowing her, it was impossible to believe for a moment that she could ever have been a thief. But as well as the photograph there was the indisputable fact that on the night of the hold-up at the Coronet Theatre she had met Sam Plant. There was no mistake about that. He had seen her in the strong light of the electric standard with his own eyes and was certain. She was on terms of intimate friendship with a notorious crook and she had lied when Jim had mentioned her being in Oxford Street, on the phone.

It was his duty to question her about that and he cast round in his mind for an opening. It was the girl herself who supplied him with one.

'What made you think I was in Oxford Street the other night?' She raised her eyes, and meeting Jim's steady gaze, blushed and looked away again.

'I thought I saw you,' he tried to speak casually. 'On my way home from the theatre.'

'What time was it when you — when you thought you saw me?' Her voice was low and he thought he detected a faint note of embarrassment in the tone.

'Nearly three o'clock — possibly a little later,' he replied.

'It couldn't have been me. I was home and in bed before twelve,' she smiled, but her eyes were worried.

Before Jim could say any more, the waiter arrived with the soup.

'Is there anything else I can get you, sir?' he asked deferentially, as he set the plates before them.

'You can come and order a wreath for yourself!' said a lugubrious voice. 'I want you, my lad!'

Jim looked up startled and saw the thin form of Sergeant Wiles standing at his elbow.

The waiter was staring at him with dropped jaw, his eyes bulging.

Wiles tapped him on the arm.

'I'll come with you while you get your coat,' he said. 'You're going a little walk with me, and don't try any tricks. I've got a pistol in my pocket. You'll have to take my word it's there because I don't want to scare all these people and put them off their food waving it about.'

'What is it, Wiles?' asked the astonished Jim. 'What's the idea?'

'The idea was a good one,' said Sergeant Wiles, tightening his grip on the waiter's arm. 'Luckily it hasn't come off. If I'd been a minute or two later, you'd have been a dead man by now, Mr. Holland. That soup's poisoned!'

'Poisoned!' Diana breathed the ominous word, horror in her eyes.

'Yes, miss, or it ought to be, unless I've made a bloomer.'

The sergeant regarded his captive sternly. 'What was it you put in that soup?' he asked.

The trembling waiter was white and silent.

'Whatever it was, the bottle's still in your pocket,' said Wiles. 'I saw you put it back there.'

The head-waiter, attracted by the scene, came up to inquire what was the matter.

His eyes opened in horrified amazement when Wiles told him.

'Good heavens, this is terrible!' he exclaimed.

Wiles nodded.

'It is,' he agreed, 'but it might have been worse. How long has this man been employed here?'

'He isn't employed here,' answered the head-waiter. 'I've never seen him until this morning and he came with a note from one of our regular waiters saying that he was ill and that this man would take his place.'

Wiles surveyed his prisoner thoughtfully.

'Who put you up to this?' he inquired.

The man showed his teeth in an unpleasant smile.

'I'm not talking,' he muttered.

Diana was white-faced and trembling

and Jim, who saw that the affair had given her a terrible shock, insisted on putting her into a taxi and sending her home. He waited until the cab drove off and then returned to Wiles. Had he remained a moment longer, he would have seen a man who had been lounging outside the Carltonian hail a second taxi and follow in the wake of the one containing the girl.

Jim accompanied the sergeant to Cannon Row police station, saw his prisoner locked in a cell, and then walked back with him to Scotland Yard. A search of the man's pockets had revealed a small blue phial, and a sniff of the contents left no shadow of doubt as to his murderous intention, for it had contained hydrocyanic acid. A portion of the soup had been carefully preserved, and when they reached headquarters Jim sent it along to the research department to be analysed.

'I was expecting something of the sort to happen,' said the melancholy sergeant a few minutes later, seated in Jim's office. 'Had a kind of hunch — I do have them at times.'

'How did you know there was anything

in that soup?' asked Jim.

'I was coming over to your table when I saw that waiter Johnnie put something in. People say there's no such thing as luck. They ought to join the police force!'

'I wonder how he knew I was going to lunch at the Carltonian?' said Jim thoughtfully. 'He must have known or he couldn't have made such elaborate plans.'

'Don't ask me,' Wiles shrugged his shoulders. 'Did you tell anyone?'

Jim shook his head.

'No,' he answered. 'Made the appointment yesterday by phone from this office.'

'Perhaps Miss Carrington told somebody?'

'Who could she have told connected with 'The Big Fellow'?' Jim stopped suddenly and was silent.

'We don't know who's connected with 'The Big Fellow', said the sergeant. He produced a foul-looking cigar and lit it with satisfaction. 'I might be for all you know and you might be for all I know. There are times when I almost suspect the Assistant Commissioner,' he added.

Jim scarcely heard him. He remembered that it had practically been Diana's own suggestion that they should lunch together. He felt a coldness round his heart at the obvious conclusion to which his thoughts were leading him. Diana Carrington was the only person besides himself who knew that he would be lunching at the Carltonian that day. Had it been she who had passed the information on to 'The Big Fellow', or alternatively had she been responsible for planning the whole diabolical scheme?

He shrank from believing it and yet common sense pointed out that it was a possible solution.

And he loved her — he no longer tried to disguise the real state of his feelings, and the knowledge made him heart sick and miserable.

'Ever heard of Florence Drew?' said Wiles suddenly.

Jim started and his eyes strayed to the locked drawer in his desk in which he had put the photograph of Diana. So Wiles knew!

'She was a wonderful woman, or rather

a girl! Pretty — I don't suppose you've ever seen a prettier — big blue eyes like a summer's sky — I always get poetical when I think of her — and skin like cream. She had the soul of a devil, but that didn't matter — nobody could see that. She looked like an angel in the dock, but that didn't stop her getting time. 'A dangerous woman', the judge called her, but he was an old man and soured.'

He paused and looked at the ceiling.

'What's all this in aid of?' snapped Jim testily.

Wiles took his eyes from the ceiling and gazed at him reproachfully.

'It isn't in aid of anything,' he said. 'I was just ruminating — and wondering. No one ever knew what became of Florence Drew. That sounds like part of a popular song, but it isn't. She had five convictions, and when she was released after the last, she disappeared. Funny if she's come back and joined 'The Big Fellow' — or maybe taken up a new profession.'

5

The Night Visitor

Leslie Venning wearily climbed the stairs — the lift was out of order — leading to his flat and, inserting his key in the lock, let himself into his comfortable chambers.

He occupied a flat on the third floor of a block in the Kingsway — a useful locality, since it was within easy distance of the law courts, an advantage to a man of his profession.

Removing his hat and coat in the tiny lobby, he walked into his sitting-room and sat down on the chesterfield drawn up in front of the gas fire with a sigh of relief.

He had spent a particularly hard day and was feeling tired.

The room in which he sat was tastefully furnished. A large grey carpet covered the floor; the walls were hidden by bookshelves, for Venning was a great reader in his spare time; the furniture was upholstered in soft brown leather, the predominating colour-scheme of the apartment.

Rising after some little time, he crossed to one of the bookcases, selected a volume, and, lighting a cigar, returned to the settee. For an hour he read and smoked, and it was nearly midnight when he finally turned out the light and went to bed. His bedroom was at the farther end of a short passage, and in ten minutes he was undressed and asleep.

He was a light sleeper and he had not been asleep for longer than an hour before he was wide awake again. Silently he got out of bed, felt in the dark for his slippers, and pulled a dressing gown round him. He took something from a drawer in his dressing-table, opened the door and crept out softly into the long hall.

The slight sound that had disturbed him had ceased. His hand was on the knob of the sitting room door and he had turned it when he heard a faint click. Someone had turned the light off within!

With a sudden motion, he flung the door wide and reached out his hand for the switch.

'Touch that light and you die!' a husky, muffled voice came from the blackness of the room. 'And drop your gun — quick!'

Venning dropped the pistol he had taken from the dressing table drawer and it fell with a thud at his feet.

'Now come inside and step lively,' went on the voice.

'Who are you?' asked Venning in a steady voice.

He strained his eyes to pierce the gloom and saw the figure dimly. It was standing by his desk.

'Never met me?' The voice was a high squeak. 'I don't suppose you have. Ever heard of 'The Big Fellow'?'

''The Big Fellow'!' Venning repeated the words dully.

'Yes.' The unknown paused. 'I want the key of your desk.'

'I haven't the key here,' said Venning. 'It's in the bedroom.'

'Don't move!' warned the voice.

Venning softly kicked off a slipper and

felt about on the floor with his bare toes for the pistol he had dropped. Presently he found it and gradually drew it towards him.

'What do you want?' he asked to gain time.

'I want to see your papers — all of them.'

'There is nothing here of any value,' said Venning.

The pistol was now at his feet. He kept his toes upon the butt ready to drop the instant an opportunity presented itself.

'Come nearer,' said the unknown, 'and hold out your hands.'

Venning made a movement as though to obey, but dropped suddenly to his knees. Grabbing the pistol, he fired. He heard a cry, saw in the flash a dark figure, and then something struck him . . .

He regained consciousness to find the light on and the room empty! His desk was open and the floor was strewn with the papers it had contained. Shakily he crossed to it and examined the lock. It had been forced. His head was aching badly and, going into the bathroom, he bathed his temples and gingerly felt the bump on the side of his forehead. Improvising a rough bandage, he returned to the disordered sitting room. The blind was flapping in the draught, for the window opening on to the back and overlooking an iron fire-escape was open.

Venning looked round grimly and picked up the telephone.

Sergeant Wiles was in his office even at that late (or early) hour, for he was preparing a report of the theatre raid when the call came through and he listened attentively while Venning explained what had happened.

'I'll come along at once — don't touch anything,' he said, and rang off.

By the time he had arrived, Venning was dressed.

'He didn't treat you any too lightly,' he remarked, eyeing the bandage, 'but it might have been worse.'

'I expected him to shoot,' said the K.C. 'He must have struck at me as I fired.'

'You say it was 'The Big Fellow' himself.' Wiles frowned. 'If it was, it's the first time he's appeared in person.'

'I'm sure it was,' said Venning. 'Look at this.' He picked up a square of paper and handed it to the sergeant.

Wiles took it and read, scrawled across the surface:

'This is your first warning. Take heed.'

It was signed 'B.F.' The detective twisted the card about in his fingers.

'Humph!' he said, after a moment's silence. 'The initials don't apply, do they? Have you any idea what the meaning of this is?'

'Not the least,' answered Venning, shrugging his shoulders.

The sergeant surveyed the disordered desk and the litter of papers on the floor with a critical eye.

'He seems to have been searching for something,' he remarked. 'Have you missed anything?'

'I haven't looked yet,' said the K.C.

'I wish you'd make sure.'

Wiles commenced a brief but thorough examination of the room, while Venning set to work sorting the papers on the desk.

It was obvious to see the way the night

visitor had got in. The iron fire-escape led down into a little backyard and the catch of the window showed a long scratch on the metal where it had been forced back.

'You didn't see the man, I suppose?' cried Wiles.

'I caught a glimpse of him as I fired. He was masked, I think.'

The sergeant nodded and continued his search of the room.

What made the burglary remarkable was the fact that the man had claimed to be 'The Big Fellow'. Never before, as far as Wiles knew, had he taken an active part in any of his operations. Why had he considered Venning worthy of his personal attention?

The K.C. had got the muddle of papers into something like order by the time Wiles had completed his investigations.

'There's nothing missing,' he declared in answer to the sergeant's question.

Wiles scratched his stubbly chin thoughtfully.

'What in the world did he come for?' he muttered perplexedly.

'Ask me another,' answered Venning.

'I'm as much puzzled as you.'

The sergeant left soon after and turned the matter over in his mind on the way back to his lodgings, but he arrived at no satisfactory solution.

In spite of the fact that he didn't go to bed until the early hours of the morning, Wiles was up betimes and was already seated in his office when Jim put in an appearance.

The young inspector looked hollow-eyed and pale.

'Any news?' he inquired, and Wiles told him of Venning's adventure of the night.

Jim Holland wrinkled his forehead.

'I wonder what his object was?' he said, unconsciously paraphrasing the sergeant's own comment of a few hours before.

'He had an object — you can bet your life on that,' answered Wiles. 'An' a pretty good one too it must have been or he wouldn't have taken the risk himself — he'd have allotted the job to one of the gang.'

The telephone rang shrilly and Wiles stretched out his arm for the instrument. After a moment's conversation, he hung up the receiver and turned to Jim with a look of satisfaction, rubbing his thin hands.

'That was Cannon Row calling,' he said cheerfully, and with the nearest approach to a smile that anyone had ever seen on his long face. 'Lynd has decided to tell all he knows.'

Jim looked puzzled for a second, then his face cleared.

'Lynd! You mean the waiter who tried to poison me?' he asked.

Wiles nodded.

'Yes, his name's Lynd,' he replied. 'I've been trying to make him talk ever since we arrested him — promised him we'd let him off lightly and get him a free passage to America. I think that's what did the trick. If he'd thought he was staying in London, he'd have remained as dumb as an oyster.'

With a feeling of expectancy, they awaited the coming of the informer, and they waited in vain.

In the company of two plainclothes men, he was taken from his cell and, with one on either side, marched round to

Scotland Yard. He looked nervous, apprehensive, and his apprehension was justified. Turning into the Whitehall entrance, his captors suddenly felt their prisoner go limp between them.

'Here! What's the matter!' exclaimed one of the detectives, as Lynd slid gently to the pavement.

A second later they both knew! Lynd was dead! Someone had shot him and the bullet passing through his heart had killed him instantly!

6

The Listener!

'They must have used a silencer,' commented Sergeant Wiles, a few minutes later, when he was told what had happened, 'and probably fired from the interior of a closed car.'

'But how did they know he was being brought here?' asked Jim. 'He'd only made up his mind to talk a few minutes before.

'How do they know anything?' replied the sergeant bitterly. 'How did they know you were going to lunch at the Carltonian?'

Jim was silent. He had his own suspicions regarding that, but Diana could have had nothing to do with this affair.

Wiles was putting on his coat.

'I'm going to make a few inquiries,' he said, in answer to Jim's question, and went out.

For some minutes after he had gone, Jim remained staring thoughtfully at his blotting pad. Then he unlocked a drawer in his desk, took out the folder containing the photograph of 'Florence Drew' and subjected it to a long and close scrutiny. There was not the slightest doubt that the girl in the photograph and Diana Carrington were one and the same. The features were identical.

Presently he arrived at a decision, for he locked the picture away again and, picking up the telephone, called Diana's number.

Her maid answered and informed him in reply to his question that her mistress was out, but that she expected her back to tea. Jim said he would call up again and turned his attention to a pile of documents and reports that required seeing to. It was routine work, dull and uninteresting, but it had to be done, and Jim was glad of the occupation, for it kept him from continual conjectures regarding the girl.

He had made up his mind. He would see Diana at the first opportunity and learn from her own lips the story concerning the photograph and the reason for her lapse into crime. That she had ever become a crook of her own free will, he steadfastly refused to believe. Somebody had a hold over her — somebody who had forced her to do their bidding against her own inclinations.

The afternoon was half over before he finished reading the last report and appended his signature. He stretched himself and was wondering whether he would find Diana at home yet if he phoned again, when Wiles came into the office.

The gaunt sergeant was looking pleased with himself.

'I've made a discovery,' he announced. 'I've found out how 'The Big Fellow' knew that Lynd was coming to put up a squeak.'

Jim looked at him in astonishment.

'When did you find this out?' he asked.

'Half an hour ago,' replied Wiles, producing the inevitable cigar and filling the office with its poisonous fumes. 'When I went out, I took a walk in the park. I can always think better when I am walking, I remember reading once — '

'Yes, yes,' said the impatient inspector. 'Never mind what you read. Go on!'

Wiles looked pained.

'I was only telling you what a beneficial effect exercise has on my constitution,' he protested.

'I don't want to hear,' said Jim Holland. 'I want to know what you've discovered.'

'Well,' went on the sergeant with a sigh, 'I was turning over in my mind this leakage of information and it seemed to me that there were only two explanations for it. One was that someone in the force had been got at, and that didn't sound reasonable when I came to think it over. And the other was the telephone!'

Jimmy Holland stared.

'The telephone!' he repeated.

Wiles nodded.

'Yes,' he said. 'Your appointment for lunch with Miss Carrington was made over the telephone and they phoned up from Cannon Row telling us about Lynd.'

'You mean the line's been tapped!'

exclaimed Jim incredulously.

'I do.' Wiles puffed vigorously at his cigar. 'As soon as I'd got the idea, I went along to the telephone people and told them my theory — I don't like the word, but I don't know another that fits — and we got busy. We found the whole bag of tricks in the top office of a building not a stone's throw away. The lines pass straight over the roof and I tell you, Mr. Holland, that there's not a word been spoken over the telephone from Scotland Yard that hasn't been listened-in to and reported to 'The Big Fellow'.'

'You got the operator?' asked the young inspector.

'You bet your life I did!' replied Wiles. 'And he's safely locked up in a cell in Cannon Row with a double guard and there he's going to stop,' he added grimly. 'If there's anything to be got out of him, we'll get it out of him there. I'm taking no more chances.'

'So that's how they knew so much,' murmured Jim softly, and a weight rolled from his heart, for the discovery exonerated Diana.

'We ought to stand a better chance now,' said Wiles. 'It won't be such a one-sided game with all the cards in the hands of the other people. We may be able to keep a few aces up our sleeves.'

'What fools we were not to have thought of it before!' said Jim. 'It was so obvious.'

'People never think of the obvious,' replied the sergeant sententiously. 'I expect 'The Big Fellow's' obvious only we can't think of him. By the way, I saw your friend Miss Carrington in the park. I never knew she was married!'

'Married!' Jim almost shouted the word in his startled surprise.

Wiles looked at him queerly.

'Didn't you know?' he asked. 'She never told you, I suppose? Women are funny like that, some of 'em, especially stage people.'

'How do you know she's married?' Jim's voice sounded strange and harsh.

'She was walking with a fellow and as I passed I heard her say: 'I can't — I'm just going to meet my husband.' Women don't say that as a rule unless they're married, or nearly so.' He scratched his chin. 'I ought to have warned her about the chap she was with,' he said. 'He's one of the biggest 'con' men in London.'

Jim Holland was silent. Diana married! He wondered why she hadn't told him. There was a mystery about the girl that seemed to deepen every day.

With a stifled sigh, he rose to his feet. His whole body ached with weariness and his eyes were hot and tired. His whole being craved for rest.

'I'm going home,' he said, putting on his coat. 'If you want me, you can give me a ring.'

Walking up Piccadilly, he suddenly remembered that he had promised to ring Diana up again and turned into a call office. The girl was still out. Coming out of the shop in which he had gone to phone, Jim almost ran into Sam Plant. The fat thief was looking extremely pleased with himself and nodded genially. He was immaculately dressed and wore a flower in his buttonhole.

'How-do-you-do, Mr. Holland!' he greeted. 'This is an unexpected pleasure.'

'Then it's all on your side,' retorted Jim shortly. 'What's the game? You look dressed to kill.'

'Tiny' Plant looked at him reproachfully.

'Don't be vulgar,' he remonstrated gently. 'There's no game. Can't a gentleman take a stroll — '

'A gentleman can, but you can't,' broke in Jim rudely. 'Listen, Plant. What were you doing in Oxford Street after the theatre hold-up?'

The crook's smile faded.

'In Oxford Street.' He shook his head. 'I wasn't in Oxford Street.'

'It's no good lying,' snapped Jim. 'I saw you myself.'

'You must have made a mistake.'

'I made no mistake, and I'd know you anywhere.' Jim Holland eyed the man steadily. 'Now come on, what were you doing?'

'You've no right to question me,' said Plant haughtily.

'We'll see about that!'

Jim looked round. A constable was strolling towards them. 'Tiny' Plant saw the direction of his glance.

'All right, I'll tell you,' he added hastily. 'If you must know, I was there to meet my wife!'

And, leaving Jim dumb with amazement, he turned on his heel and hurried away.

7

Murder!

Sam Plant walked rapidly along in the direction of Piccadilly Circus and every now and again he broke into a little chuckle. He had certainly scored off James Holland and the thought filled him with satisfaction.

And it was not only this that gave him so much enjoyment. He was keeping an appointment that evening, the result of which, if it worked out as he anticipated, should put him in possession of a fortune. The matter required careful handling, but 'Tiny' flattered himself that he was capable of that.

He had over an hour to fill in somehow, and turning into a well-known restaurant, he managed after some difficulty to find a vacant table and ordered tea.

He finished his tea and sat on, his mind occupied by pleasant thoughts of the future. If what he expected happened, he need never work again — not that 'Tiny' had ever worked in his adventurous life, but he called it that — it sounded better! At last it was time to go, and, paying his bill, fee strolled out.

The commissionaire called him a taxi and, stepping in, he was driven to Marble Arch. He paid the driver and walked through the big gates into the park. He was one minute too early for his appointment and paced slowly along the unfrequented path that runs parallel with Park Lane.

The minutes passed, two . . . three . . . and still the person he was expecting failed to put in an appearance.

A frown of annoyance wrinkled Sam Plant's smooth brow. He disliked being kept waiting. He told himself that he would have something to say about it. Ten minutes went by. The frown was replaced by a slight expression of uneasiness. Supposing no one turned up? He dismissed the thought. It was impossible with such a lot at stake, but he hated being treated with contempt like this.

After twenty minutes' walking up and down and nothing had happened, he made his way into Oxford Street and sought a telephone at the Tube station. But the exchange told him there was no reply from the number he called.

Fuming with rage, he stood on the edge of the pavement, trying to make up his mind what to do next. There seemed nothing for it but to go home. He decided on this in the end after one last glance in the park.

Sam Plant possessed a smart flat in Maida Vale. It was a tiny place, but it was comfortably, even luxuriously furnished, and it served his needs.

There was no lift — 'Tiny' had chosen this particularly because he wanted privacy and disliked his comings and goings to be under the eye of a porter — and, mounting the stairs, he opened the door with his latchkey and slipped into the hall. The place was in darkness, which rather surprised him, and he felt along the wall for the switch. Pressing it down, he removed his hat and coat and hung them up. The sitting room door was ajar and, pushing it open, he flooded the place with light. The next moment he started back with a cry of horror.

★　★　★

Jim Holland stared after the rapidly retreating figure of 'Tiny' Plant, incapable of movement, his mind in a whirl. Diana was this man's wife! It sounded incredible and yet, unless it were true, the crook could have had no object in making the statement. Taken in conjunction with what Sergeant Wiles had told him, there seemed little room for doubt.

With a supreme effort, Jim pulled his shattered brains together and walked on. He was feeling unutterably miserable. The whole bottom had fallen out of existence and there seemed to be a leaden weight in his inside.

He moved unconsciously, hardly aware of his surroundings, curiously dead and apathetic. How long he walked about up one street and down another he never knew, but presently he found himself outside the Coronet Theatre.

A sudden intense desire to see Diana took possession of him. The audience were already going in and, making his way round to the stage-door, he inquired for her at the keeper's box.

The man shook his head.

'Miss Carrington's not here tonight, sir,' he said. 'Her understudy's playing. She sent a message to say she was ill.'

Jim thanked him and turned away. He had a vague idea of going to her flat at Victoria, but gave it up and eventually decided to go home.

He was feeling thoroughly ill. Lack of sleep and the strain of the last months were taking effect. He forced himself to regard the whole matter calmly and by the time he reached his flat had regained something at any rate of his normal composure.

He made a pretence of eating the appetizing dinner Punt had prepared, and he had just finished when the telephone rang. Jim felt so tired that he had half a mind not to answer the call and then, thinking that it might be from headquarters and something important, he unhooked the receiver.

A hoarse, strained voice came over the wire.

'Is that Holland? For God's sake come round to my place at once!'

'Who's speaking?' said Jim sharply.

'Plant,' was the reply, and so changed was his voice that Jim failed to recognize the slightest resemblance to 'Tiny's' usual tones. 'A terrible thing has happened. You will come?'

'Where are you?' asked the young inspector.

'At my fiat,' said Plant. 'Fourteen Luverdale Mansions. Don't waste time talking — come!'

'Why, what's happened?'

'Murder!' The voice choked over the word. 'For the love of heaven come quickly!'

Jim heard the click as the receiver was hung up, dragged on his overcoat, and, hurrying into the street, hailed a passing taxi. In less than twenty minutes he was deposited at the entrance to Luverdale Mansions.

Sam Plant opened the door himself in

response to Jim's summons and the young inspector thought he had never seen such a change in a man. The fat, usually florid face was pale and in some peculiar way seemed to have fallen in. The skin hung in loose bags beneath the eyes and round the heavy jaw. 'Tiny' Plant looked like a man who had received sentence of death.

'It was good of you to come so quickly,' he said huskily, as Jim stepped into the passage, and without further word he led the way across to a door on the right.

'Look!' he said, and pointed a shaking hand into the room beyond.

Jim looked, and looking drew in his breath with a sharp hiss.

The room was in the utmost disorder. Drawers had been hurriedly pulled open and their contents tipped in a heap on the floor. Even the carpet had been rolled back. The place had been subjected to a thorough search. And then he saw something else. Over by the fireplace lay the body of a woman!

With a heart that for a second almost

stopped beating, Jim walked quickly over and bent down.

The next moment he started back with a great cry.

It was Diana, and the knife that had killed her still protruded from her breast!

8

The Button

Jim Holland's face went white and the whole room swam before his eyes. Diana . . . dead . . .

He steadied himself by clutching the back of a chair and for the first time in his life felt almost on the verge of fainting. By a supreme effort of will, however, he managed to pull himself together and turned to Sam Plant.

'When did this happen?' he asked in a voice that startled him — it was so unlike his own, so dead and lifeless.

'While I was out,' said 'Tiny', in a hushed whisper.

'My God, how dreadful!' Jim forced himself to look again at the dead girl. He remembered the first night at the Coronet. How sparkling and full of vitality she had been! 'She'll never act again,' he muttered aloud, and his eyes were blurred.

'What do you mean?' He heard Plant's voice as though from a long way off. 'You're making a mistake, aren't you?'

'A mistake?' said Jim vaguely. 'No, there's no mistake. I wish to God there were!'

'You think — that it's Diana, don't you?' asked Plant unsteadily. 'Well, you're wrong!'

'Wrong!' Jim swung round and gripped the man by the arm. 'She *is* Diana!'

'Tiny' Plant shook his head sadly.

'She isn't,' he replied. 'I'd give all I possess in the world if she were, but she isn't.'

'But — ' stammered Jim, and stopped — his throat was so dry that the words wouldn't come.

'She was my wife — Florence Drew — Diana's twin sister,' said Plant huskily.

A great light broke suddenly on Jim. Florence Drew — the original of the photograph in the record department at the Yard — Diana's twin sister. The intense relief almost overwhelmed him. He lowered his shaking limbs into a chair.

'It was Florence Drew I saw you with in Oxford Street,' he said, and 'Tiny' inclined his head. 'I see.' He paused and, seeing the bowed head of the other, stretched out his hand impulsively. 'I'm terribly sorry, Plant.'

The jewel thief grasped the extended palm and gripped it.

'Thank you,' he muttered simply.

For some time there was a dead silence.

'Tell me,' said Jim at last, 'do you know who was responsible for — this?' He looked in the direction of the hearth.

'I do.' 'Tiny' Plant's voice was harsh. 'And if it takes me all the rest of my life, I'll get him for it.'

'Who was it?'

' "The Big Fellow"!' Plant breathed the name from between set teeth and his hands clenched until the knuckles showed white and prominent.

'But why?' asked Jim. 'What was his object? What reason had he for the crime?'

The crook hesitated.

'I can't tell you that,' he said after a

pause. 'But it was a good one — the best reason of all.'

Jim raised his eyes and met the other's glance. Something in that set face told him that the man was on the verge of a nervous collapse.

'Do you know him?'

Again Plant hesitated.

'Yes,' he said, and his voice was almost inaudible, 'I know him! But I'm not going to tell you, Holland, so it's no good asking me. You wouldn't believe me if I did and I've got no proof. He's as clever as the devil. But I'll get him' — his throat cracked — 'for what he's done to Florence — if I'm still alive!' he ended grimly.

'If you're still alive?' repeated Jim quickly. 'Do you believe you're in danger then?'

'I know I'm in danger,' said 'Tiny', 'the greatest possible danger, but I'm taking precautions.'

Jim tried to persuade him to say more, but the man was adamant. He gave it up at last and turned his attention to the disordered flat. Sam Plant had had to go out to a call-office to ring him up, for the telephone was not working, and Jim discovered the cause when he found the neatly-severed lead-in wire. It had been cut close to the front door. There were signs in the passage of a struggle and it was fairly easy to see how the murderer had gained access to the flat. He had simply rung the bell in the ordinary way and when Florence Drew had opened the door, had forced his way in. Jim searched the whole place carefully, but without result. Plant had recovered a little from his first shattering grief by the time he had finished, though he talked and moved like a man dead inside, with a sort of dull, lifeless apathy that was a more poignant indication of his suffering than the greatest outburst.

Jim sent him out to ring up the nearest police station.

When an inspector and the divisional surgeon arrived, he briefly explained the situation and, putting the man in charge, prepared to take his leave.

'Tiny' Plant accompanied him to the door and Jim paused on the threshold.

'Are you staying here tonight?' he asked, and Plant shook his head.

'Where are you going?'

'Anywhere — an hotel probably,' said 'Tiny', 'anywhere but here. I couldn't stay here.' He shivered.

It was at that moment that Jim saw the button. It was lying by the hall-stand close up against the wall and he would never have noticed it but for the fact that he was standing in just the right position to catch the reflected light from its shiny surface.

Going back, he stooped quickly and picked it up.

'Is this — ' he was beginning and broke off sharply, for he recognized it!

It was an overcoat button with a peculiar design stamped on the face — a clenched hand — and Jim drew in his breath swiftly as he looked at it. For it belonged to Harry Littleton!

9

The Record

Jim Holland arrived at his office in Scotland Yard early on the following morning, feeling more cheerful than he had done for many days past. The discovery that Diana had no connection with the photograph and that all his half-formed suspicions were without cause, had done much to bring about this optimistic outlook.

His first action on reaching the Yard was to lock the button in his safe. It was a damning piece of evidence and if it could be relied on, there was no need to look any further than Harry Littleton for the unknown murderer.

Jim sat down at his desk and gazed thoughtfully at the blotting paper in front of him. If it had been Littleton who had killed Florence Drew, then he was also 'The Big Fellow'!

He pulled the telephone towards him and rang up the reporter.

Twenty minutes later a smiling Harry was shown into his office.

Jim checked his flow of questions and fetching his button from his safe held it out.

'Is this yours?' he inquired.

Littleton leant forward and peered at it.

'Yes' he said in wonder. 'How in the world did you come by it?'

'A woman was murdered last night,' said Jim quietly, 'a woman named Florence Drew.' He watched Harry keenly. 'She was killed in a flat belonging to Sam Plant some time between the hours of four-thirty and eight. I found this button in the passage.'

The reporter's face went pale.

'Good God, Jim,' he exclaimed, 'you surely don't suspect me!'

'It's your button,' Jim replied meaningfully.

'But I lost it two days ago,' protested the reporter.

'Then how did it get in Sam Plant's flat? Have you ever been there?'

'Never in my life,' said Harry emphatically. 'Besides, I can prove that I had no hand in the affair. If this woman was killed between the hours you say, I couldn't have had anything to do with it. I was at the *Megaphone* offices from four until after eight. Ring up old 'Baldy' — he'll tell you.'

Jim got through to the *Megaphone* and spoke to the news-editor. The conversation was brief and he hung up the receiver and turned to Harry.

'He bears out all you say,' he said with a puzzled frown. 'Your alibi's cast iron. But how on earth did the button get there? I suppose you can't remember where you lost it?'

Harry shook his head.

'I haven't the least idea,' he replied.

'It seems almost too great a coincidence to believe that the person who killed Florence Drew could have been wearing a coat with identical buttons,' said Jim thoughtfully.

'It's totally impossible,' said Harry. 'When I found I'd lost it, I went to the tailor who made the coat and asked him to put on another. But he said he couldn't match it. It's an American button and there are no others in England except the few he used up on my coat.' He picked up the button which Jim had laid on his desk and looked at it. 'There's no doubt about it being mine.'

He could offer no suggestion as to how the button had got into the hall of 'Tiny' Plant's flat, and presently took his leave. Nothing very much happened during the day, but there were many odd jobs to be done, and it was not until quite late that Jim was able to leave the Yard and go home. He was feeling very tired, and when he had eaten the supper which Punt brought to him on a tray, he sat down and wrote to Diana. He stamped the letter and sent the man out with it, and settled down before the fire for a final cigarette. He was interrupted by the return of Punt who came into the room and laid a flat package on the table.

'What's that?' asked Jim sitting up.

The servant shook his head with a puzzled frown.

'I don't know, sir,' he answered. 'I

found it on the step when I came back from the post. It wasn't there when I went out.'

Jim picked it up.

'It's addressed to me all right,' he said and began to tear off the wrappings.

Inside, packed between two sheets of stout cardboard, was a gramophone record. It was a thin metal disk of the kind that is used for home recording, and there was nothing to indicate what it was, nor, although he searched carefully, was there any line of writing with it.

'Extraordinary!' muttered Jim in amazement. 'I suppose we'd better play the thing and see what it's all about. Probably an advertisement of some kind.'

He possessed a gramophone — a seldom-used portable — and, fetching it from a corner, placed the record on the turntable and started the motor. A voice, high-pitched and squeaky, started speaking and at the first words Jim Holland went tense and his face set.

'You have refused to leave me alone,' it said, 'and you have been lucky to have escaped with your life. In future, you can rest in peace, for I shall not attempt to kill you again. I have thought of a better way. I have taken someone who is very dear to you, and if you ever wish to see her again, you will cease all further efforts to track me down. Diana Carrington is in my hands and unless you agree to my terms, she will die. This is no idle threat, so be warned.'

The voice stopped and only the scratching of the needle on the surface of the record broke the silence.

For a moment Jim was stunned, then he rushed at the telephone and rang up the stage-door of the Coronet Theatre.

'Miss Carrington left ten minutes ago,' came the reply to his question, and Jim banged the receiver back in despair.

And at that precise moment, Diana was lying back unconscious in the interior of a big limousine car and being driven she knew not whither by the man who crouched over the wheel!

10

The Warehouse

It was a little after half-past eleven when Diana left the theatre and, deciding to walk home, turned up Shaftesbury Avenue.

Her way home led her through Wardour Street to Leicester Square and she noticed, without any particular interest, that a large black-painted limousine that had been standing outside the theatre when she came out was purring softly along in her wake.

Crossing the road, she turned into Whitcombe Street and from thence into Orange Street. She had proceeded half-way along this street when she saw the black car pass her and draw into the kerb. Still without any premonition of coming danger, she continued on her way, and then suddenly, as she drew level with the limousine, something was thrown over her head and she felt herself seized in a pair of strong hands!

She tried to cry out, but the thickness of the cloth that swathed her head choked the sound. In spite of her struggles, she was dragged into the car, and the enveloping cloth was whisked from her head, to be replaced by a pad of something that was pressed heavily over her nose and mouth! A sickly, overpowering odour filled her nostrils, and, guessing what it was, she tried desperately to hold her breath. For what seemed an eternity she succeeded, and then her tortured lungs refused to be denied the air they needed any longer. She gave a sobbing, strangled gasp . . . felt her senses reel . . . and slipped into oblivion.

★   ★   ★

How long Diana remained unconscious she never knew, but her first waking sensation was one of physical sickness. It was accompanied by a violent throbbing in her temples and her mouth and throat felt dry and hot. She would have given everything she possessed at that moment for a cup of strong tea . . .

For some time she felt too dazed and ill to take much notice of her surroundings, but after a while the throbbing in her head abated a little and she opened her eyes and looked about her. She could see nothing; wherever she was, she was in pitch darkness. Presently she discovered the reason for the hot, dry sensation in her mouth, for, trying to pass her tongue over her parched lips, she found that something soft had been thrust into her mouth and tied there securely. She had been gagged! She tried to raise her hands to pull the thing away and found that she had been bound as well. A tentative movement of her legs convinced her that they also had been securely tied.

Where was she and who had been responsible for her kidnapping? She could find no answer to these questions, but presently she became aware of a familiar smell that permeated the atmosphere. At first she couldn't place it, and then it dawned on her that it was petrol! She was lying half propped up against a leather cushion — she could tell it was leather by the feel of it against her face — and, after a moment or two's puzzling, she came to the conclusion that she was still in the car.

But where was the car? It was no longer in motion or even in the open. The truth came to her in a flash. It was in a garage!

She had reached this stage in her conjectures when the grating of a key in a lock came to her ears, followed by the squeak of hinges, and then a pencil of light cut through the blackness. It wavered for a moment and then went out, but it had been sufficient to confirm her belief that she was still in the black limousine.

The light flashed on again and she saw vaguely a dark figure lean over the driving seat of the car and fumble under the dashboard. The headlights sprang radiance, throwing two white circles on a pair of double doors that stood ajar a few feet in front of them. In the reflected light she saw the figure of a man enveloped in a heavy motor coat come round to the side of the car and, opening the door, peer in at her. He evidently saw that she had recovered consciousness, for he gave a grunt and a nod and, without further comment, flung a heavy suitcase in beside her. She couldn't see his face, for it was concealed by an enormous pair of goggles, and he wore a slouch hat pulled low, so that the broad brim met the mica eye-pieces.

There was something about him that terrified her. Who was he and what was he going to do with her?

Her second question was quickly answered, for, slamming the door, he walked round to the front of the car and pushed the garage doors wide. Coming back, he climbed into the driving seat and took his place behind the wheel.

Diana felt the car shiver as the powerful engine started and they began to move slowly forward. They went about fifty yards and then the unknown stopped the car, got down and went back. She heard the thud as he shut the doors of the garage and the jingle of keys. A second later he was back in the car and with a jerk it started forward once more, swung sharply to the right and, gathering speed, went humming off into the night.

Diana's heart was thumping so hard that she could hear it above the throb of the machine. She had gone icy cold with fear when that sinister figure had appeared at the window, but now her terror was so great that she almost fainted . . .

What lay at the end of this mad ride? Where were they bound for? She twisted her head so that she could look out of the window, but she could see nothing but blackness and the occasional flash of light from a passing lamppost. The route they were following seemed to be a particularly tortuous one, for the limousine twisted first to the left, then to the right, and then to the left again in a bewildering number of turns and corners. She concluded — and rightly — that her mysterious captor was trying to avoid the main thoroughfares and was going to this unknown destination by means of back streets.

Twice they crossed a broad road and she felt the car bump over tram-lines and then, after what seemed an age, she saw that they were running down a street by the side of a high wall, above which, in the spluttering light of arc standards, she made out dimly the outlines of tall buildings and huge cranes . . . She heard the muffled hoot of a siren close at hand and realized that they must be close to the river. Almost at the same time she became aware of a steady, staccato throbbing behind her and, after a great deal of trouble, managed to twist herself round until her eyes were on a level with the small window at the back of the limousine. The blind had been drawn down, but there was a narrow crack at the bottom through which she could see. A hundred yards behind a powerful light was following, dancing up and down as the motorcycle to which it was attached bumped over the uneven surface of the road.

Diana drew in her breath quickly and a flood of hope filled her heart. Had someone seen her abduction and followed . . . ? Could it be Jim . . . ? For one wild moment she thought it might be, but the next she had dismissed the idea as impossible.

The car swung round to the left sharply and for a second she caught a glimpse of a policeman standing on the corner before the shock flung her to one side.

The steady plop-plop of the motor-cycle exhaust was coming nearer and she saw the machine flash into view alongside the limousine. The driver shouted something, his hand went up and she saw a flash and heard a report. Then to her horror the man behind the wheel of the car leaned out and she caught sight of the squat shape of an automatic in his hand. A second report rang out, she heard a choked cry, and the motorcycle wobbled, ran on a few yards and crashed into the kerb . . .

The driver of the limousine gave a short laugh and sent the car bounding forward at increased speed. They skidded round another corner into a narrow, mean little street, raced dawn it and came out into a broader highway. They proceeded for a short distance along this and then, with a grinding of brakes, the unknown brought the car to a halt opposite a pair of high wooden gates.

He slipped down quickly from his seat, hurried over to the gates and she heard the chink of metal against metal and presently saw the gates swing inwards.

Coming back to the car, he backed it and swung it round until the long radiator pointed at the opening, and then drove it into what appeared to be a courtyard.

Stopping the engine, he switched off the lights and, going round the back of the car, she heard him close and relock the gates. Diana's heart was heavy with despair. The faint hope that had come to her with the appearance of the motor-cyclist had faded and she felt half-dead with fear.

The unknown came to the side of the car and jerked open the door. Leaning forward, he gathered her up in his arms and lifted her out. She saw the towering bulk of huge buildings rising into the darkness on all sides, caught a glimpse of twinkling lights, and heard the swish-swish of lapping water, before he carried her swiftly through a narrow doorway, along a pitch-dark and evil-smelling passage, and finally deposited her none too gently on a hard floor. There came the sound of a scraping match and after a short interval the feeble yellow light of a candle flickered. She looked about her and in the tiny glimmer saw that she was in a big, barn-like room littered with rubbish and broken packing-cases, on one of which the candle had been stuck.

The man who had brought her to this dismal place came over and stood looking down at her for a moment in silence, then he spoke.

'You've got Jim Holland to thank for this,' he said harshly. 'If it hadn't been for his damned meddling, I shouldn't have had to resort to this method of safeguarding myself.'

She stared up at the sinister figure above her with frightened eyes. What did he mean? Who was he? And why was Jim to blame for her abduction?

It almost seemed as if he could read her thoughts, for he answered her unspoken questions immediately.

'I don't know how much Holland

knows or guesses,' he continued, 'but I'm not taking any chances. But if he becomes troublesome, I can play you as my trump card. He'll be willing to shut his eyes to a lot to get you safely back.' He stopped and walked over to the door. 'So you'd better make yourself as comfortable as you can because you're likely to stay here for a long time. This place is empty and I hold the lease, so there's not the slightest chance of you being found. I'll come down every night and bring you some food.'

He stood on the threshold and regarded her with a hard smile playing about his mouth.

'And if you try to escape,' he grated menacingly, 'I'll serve you as I served your sister and her precious husband.'

He went out, leaving the girl shivering with fear. Everything was clear now. This man was the ringleader. And she was helpless in his clutches! If only her hands and feet were free . . . The thought made her strain at the cords that secured her wrists and her heart bounded as she felt them give slightly. She had been wearing thick gloves when she left the theatre and her captor had not troubled to remove them before binding her hands. If she could get her hands out . . .

Desperately she tugged and by degrees began to shift the cords until they slipped over the top of her gloves on to her bare wrists. They were loose now and after a little trouble she succeeded in pulling off one of her gloves and dragging one hand free! She paused breathlessly, listening, but all was silent and after a moment she sat up and, leaning forward, began to tear at the knots that secured her ankles . . . She broke her nails and hurt her fingers, but she managed to untie them and rose shakily to her feet. Her legs, numbed by the impeded circulation, almost gave way under her, and she had to hold on to a packing-case for support.

As she rubbed them gently, she prayed that the man might not come back and catch her. For the moment she was free, and if only he would stay away a little longer, she might find a way of escape.

Presently she found that she was able to walk and crept over to the door. She listened on the threshold, but there was no sound, and with her heart thumping painfully in her breast, she began to feel her way carefully along the dark passage. The narrow door at the end was ajar and she cautiously pushed it further open and slipped out into the courtyard. The car was still standing there, but there was no sign of the man. He must be still somewhere about, she concluded, otherwise the car would have gone. She looked swiftly about her. The gates by which they had entered were locked and were too high for her to think of climbing them. She decided to try the other direction and made her way towards what she guessed was a wharf, for she could hear faintly the sound of rushing water. In the distance twinkled a row of uneven lights and from close at hand came the melancholy wail of a siren.

Diana concluded that she was close to the river and at that moment a dark figure loomed up in front of her! She heard a startled exclamation and, dodging the hands thrust out to grasp her, ran blindly forward . . .

'Come back, you fool . . . '

The hoarse voice was close behind her . . . She heard the thud of his pursuing footsteps. Capture seemed inevitable and she redoubled her speed . . . She felt the touch of fingers on her arm and made one wild leap to escape his outstretched hands . . . Her feet suddenly trod on nothing and before she could recover her balance, she was falling . . . falling . . . She struck ice-cold water with a splash, was caught by a swiftly moving current arid whirled round in an eddy. Dimly, as the water closed over her head and roared in her ears, she heard a shout . . . and lost consciousness.

11

A Message from Plant

Jim Holland, grey-faced and drawn, met Sergeant Wiles outside the theatre.

'We've got to find her,' he said brokenly, between his teeth. 'We've got to!'

The sergeant nodded. He was talking to a big man, hat-less and wearing a rough bandage round his head.

'I've got a description of the car she was taken in,' he said, and Jim looked bewildered. 'This is Detective-Constable Hodgson,' continued Wiles, 'and he saw the whole thing happen — tried to prevent it as a matter of fact, but was laid out.'

'It was a big limousine,' said the man, 'a Spange. I was following Miss Carrington — '

'Following her?' broke in Jim.

'Yes, sir,' said the man. 'I've been

following her for days — on Sergeant Wiles's instructions.'

Jim caught Wiles's eye and understood. He also had seen the photograph in Records and mistaken Diana for Florence Drew.

'She left the theatre after the performance and was walking down a side street,' the detective continued, 'when the car drew up to the kerb. I'd seen it before during the evening, but hadn't taken much notice. A man sprang out; threw a cloth over the young lady's head and dragged her into the car. It was all done in a flash. I ran forward to interfere when I realized what was happening, but before I'd taken three steps, something came down on my head and I don't remember any more.'

'We ought to be able to trace the car,' said Jim. 'There aren't many Spanges on the road.'

He felt desperately ill, but was trying his hardest to keep calm. He knew that the only hope was to force himself to think as clearly as possible. It was only by clear thinking and quick action that he had the ghost of a chance of finding Diana.

Wiles had telephoned to the Yard directly he heard Hodgson's story and a description of the car had been circulated to all stations with orders to hold and detain the driver and occupants. Considering that barely fifteen minutes had passed since Jim had rung him up with the story of the record, the melancholy sergeant had certainly not wasted his time.

Hodgson went off to have his head properly dressed and Jim and Wiles drove to Scotland Yard. Sitting in Jim's office, they waited for news to come through.

'I didn't tell you I'd put anyone on to watch Miss Carrington,' said Wiles, breaking a long silence. 'I thought maybe you'd be annoyed.'

'I'm glad you did as it turns out,' said Jim, rising and starting to pace up and down. 'Good God, this waiting's terrible!'

'We can't do anything else,' replied Wiles philosophically. He fished in an inner pocket (he was still wearing his dilapidated mackintosh) and found one of the inevitable cigars. 'I don't think the girl's in any immediate danger,' he went on, biting off the end and carefully lighting it. 'It wouldn't do him any good to harm her. His scheme is to hold her as a hostage until he's got clean away. He's playing now for his own safety. He's not quite sure how much we know and by taking the girl he thinks that if the worst comes to the worst, he'll be able to bargain with us.'

There was a lot of truth in what he said and Jim knew it, though it did little to mitigate the almost unbearable feeling of utter helplessness that he felt.

The time dragged slowly by and still he paced up and down the worn carpet, staring fixedly in front of him and trying to force his weary brain to think of something, some method that would enable him to trace Diana . . .

It was nearly two o'clock when the telephone bell shrilled insistently and Wiles pulled the instrument towards him.

'Hello — yes!' he growled, and then Jim, watching eagerly, saw his face change as he listened to a long conversation from the other end of the wire. 'All right — yes — we'll be there in about a quarter of an hour.'

He hung up the receiver and turned to his impatient companion.

'That was from the Divisional Inspector of K. Division,' he said. 'A police patrol picked up 'Tiny' Plant in a dying condition half an hour ago in a side turning off the East India Dock road. He'd been shot! He says he's got a statement to make and wants to see you.' The sergeant rose to his feet. 'I said we'd go right along at once. They don't think he'll live very long.'

'Good God!' gasped Jim. 'Plant! I wonder who shot him?'

'That's what I'd like to know.' Wiles transferred the chewed butt of his cigar from one side of his mouth to the other with a rolling motion of his lips. 'I've got an idea that he'll be able to tell us something about Miss Carrington.'

'Why?' demanded Jim in surprise, as he followed the sergeant to the door.

'Don't know — just an idea,' replied Wiles.

Ten minutes later, they were tearing through the night, bound for the station from which the call had come.

The fast police car that Wiles had had ready and waiting ate up the distance, for there existed no traffic regulations for them, and in a little over twenty minutes they drew up outside their destination.

The inspector in charge had evidently been looking out for them and came down the steps to the side of the car almost before it had stopped moving.

'We took him to the infirmary, sir,' he said in answer to Wiles's question. 'He was very badly injured, shot through the stomach. You'll have to hurry. I don't think he'll live very long.'

The melancholy sergeant made room for him as he climbed into the car beside him.

'How did it happen?' asked Jim, after the inspector had given a few instructions to the driver and they shot away with a jerk. 'Who shot him?'

The inspector shook his head.

'Don't know, sir,' he replied briefly. 'It was a mysterious affair altogether. Police

Constable Cooke, the man who found him, says that he was standing at the top of Lime Street when a big car passed him going at a fair speed. It was followed by a motorcycle. Cooke watched them as they turned down the street and about half-way along the motorcycle caught up with the car and drew alongside. The next moment Cooke heard the sound of two shots and the driver of the motorcycle fell into the roadway, his machine on the top of him. The big car tore off and disappeared down a side street.'

'Did Cooke get the number?' snapped Jim excitedly.

'No, sir,' said the inspector. 'He said he couldn't because there was a streak of mud across the plate. If the car hadn't been going at such a speed, he'd have pulled it up for that.'

'Does he know what make it was?' asked Wiles, and the inspector nodded.

'Yes,' he answered, 'he says it was a Spange — a black limousine.'

'That's our car!' cried Jim, and his heart gave a bound. 'Why didn't Cooke stop it in the first place? You must have got the hurry call to pull up and detain the occupants of a black Spange limousine .'

'We did, sir,' said the inspector, a trifle stiffly, 'but Cooke didn't know anything about that. The instructions didn't come through until after he'd left the station for duty. The sergeant would have told him when he met him on his rounds, but this happened before.'

'I see.' Jim spoke bitterly. It was galling to know that the car he would have given ten years of his life to find had actually been almost within their grasp. And Diana —

His thoughts were mercifully interrupted by the police car pulling up outside the infirmary. They got out hurriedly and followed the inspector into the vestibule.

A few seconds later they were joined by the doctor in charge, a short, bespectacled man who approached them wearing a grave expression on his rather florid face.

'I'm afraid you're too late, gentlemen,'

he said when the inspector had introduced them. 'The man died three minutes ago!'

Jim felt a great wave of despair pass over him. Unconsciously perhaps, he had set his hopes of finding Diana on this interview with the wounded crook and now —

With a supreme effort of will, however, he regained control of himself, and when he spoke his voice was cool and steady.

'Didn't he leave any message — make any statement before he died?' he asked.

To his surprise, for his question had been more in the nature of a forlorn hope than anything else, the doctor nodded.

'Yes,' he replied. 'He asked for a pencil and paper and wrote a note to be given to you. It's in my office. If you'll wait here a moment, I'll get it.'

He bustled away, returning after a short interval carrying an envelope.

Jim saw his name scrawled in almost illegible characters across it and, with hands that shook in spite of all his efforts to keep them steady, tore open the flap and extracted the contents.

As he read the last message from 'Tiny' Plant, a name leapt out from among the wavering writing and danced before his eyes as though traced in letters of fire.

'Good God!' he breathed, and thrust the sheet of paper into Wiles's hand, his face blank with amazement.

For the identity of 'The Big Fellow' was a mystery no longer and the revelation had given Jim Holland one of the greatest surprises he had ever experienced in his life!

12

The Big Fellow

Jim Holland accompanied Sergeant Wiles and the Divisional Inspector back to the police station in a frame of mind that can only be described as chaotic. The revelation of 'The Big Fellow's' identity had reduced him to a state of mind that was neither amazement nor incredulity, but a mixture of both.

Wiles had taken the discovery with his usual philosophical calmness and the faintest possible lift to his shaggy brows.

'Surprised?' he remarked, when Jim commented on his lack of emotion. 'You can't surprise me. If 'The Big Fellow' had turned out to be the Prime Minister himself, I shouldn't have been surprised. The only thing that might astonish me would be if I backed a horse and it won!'

He phoned through to Scotland Yard from the inspector's office and five minutes after he had ceased speaking, twenty Flying Squad tenders left the grim building on the Thames Embankment to spread in all directions searching for the man whose name and description the melancholy sergeant had given them over the wire.

The inspector brought them hot coffee and then went off to attend, to the preliminaries connected with the murder of 'Tiny' Plant and to write out his report. Jim drank the steaming fluid gratefully. His face was white and haggard and he felt half-dead with anxiety and fatigue.

Although they now knew the name of the man who had been responsible for Diana's abduction, it brought them no nearer to finding the girl nor gave them the slightest clue as to her whereabouts.

By now she might be miles away. The only grain of comfort that eased his tortured mind was the conviction that the girl was, at the moment at any rate, not in any actual danger. He was too clever to injure her in any way, for that would only defeat his own object. But this helplessness, this enforced inaction was terribly nerve-racking.

'Isn't there anything else we can do?' burst out Jim, after they had sat in silence for ten minutes.

Wiles removed the inevitable cigar he had lighted from his mouth and shook his head.

'I don't see what,' he replied dolefully. 'It's no good us chasin' about lookin' for a black limousine when we don't know where to look. Besides, every p'liceman in the country's on the watch by now and the Squad as well. If that car's above ground, they'll find it sooner or later. All we can do is to go back to the Yard and wait for news.'

He looked at his superior critically.

'And if I was you,' he added, 'I'd go along home and try and get some sleep.'

Jim uttered an impatient exclamation.

'Sleep!' he cried. 'Damn it all, do you think I *could* sleep!'

'I said 'try',' the sergeant pointed out patiently. 'It's no good worryin' yerself sick. 'Mens what-do-yer-callum in corpus something-or-other.' You know what I mean.'

''*Mens sana in corpore sano*',' said Jim mechanically.

'That's it — I never was much of a French scholar,' said Wiles with unconscious humour. 'Means that if you're feelin' fit, your brain works better. It was Luke Hanson, the American 'con' man, who told me that, and 'e ought to have known what 'e was talkin' about. A cleverer — '

The telephone rang and stopped the sergeant's rambling, to Jim's unspeakable relief, and Wiles pulled the instrument towards him.

'Yes?' he grunted. 'What is it?'

There was a brief conversation from the person at the other end and then Wiles looked over at Jim.

'Just a minute,' he said. 'Sergeant Yarle, of the Thames Police, wants to speak to you,' he went on to Jim. 'He's been on to the Yard and they told him to try here.'

The young inspector was at the telephone before he had finished speaking.

'Hello!' he cried. 'Yes — Inspector Holland speaking. What's that?' He listened while the speaker talked rapidly and then: 'Right, hold on a moment.' He turned to Wiles, his eyes shining. 'They've found Diana,' he exclaimed. 'Picked her out of the river in a police launch at Limehouse Reach. She was unconscious and wearing a gag when they found her, but she recovered almost at once and asked for me. Yarle says she either jumped or was thrown from a wharf. He hasn't had time to question her yet.'

'Ask him what wharf it was,' said the sergeant quickly, and Jim turned once more to the telephone.

'It was the wharf belonging to a disused warehouse between Albert Wharf and Buxham Wharf,' he announced a few seconds later, hanging up the receiver.

'Good!' snapped Wiles. 'Where was Yarle phoning from?'

'Limehouse Reach T.P. Station,' replied Jim, and his weariness seemed to have vanished like magic. 'I'm going along there at once.'

'I'll come with you,' said the sergeant,

and picked up the phone, giving a Treasury number. 'Hello!' he called. 'Detective-Sergeant Wiles speaking. Put me through to Flying Squad control department.' There was a moment's pause and then: 'Hello! Wiles this end. Rush all Squad cars to Limehouse. Tell 'em to throw a cordon round the empty warehouse situated between Albert Wharf and Buxham's. I'll attend to the river end. Right!' He slapped down the receiver.

'Now I'm ready,' he said, and they hurried out to the waiting police car.

A thin drizzle of rain was falling, but they didn't wait to put up the hood. Jim gave some hasty directions to the driver and they shot off, heading for Limehouse Causeway, and while and from all points of the they sped along the nearly-deserted streets, a man in the wireless control tower at Scotland Yard was flashing Wiles's message through the night to the patrolling cars of the Flying Squad compass they began to converge, racing towards the disused warehouse on the left-hand bank of Limehouse Reach.

It took Jim and the sergeant five

minutes to reach their destination and before the car had come to a standstill the young inspector had sprung out and was tearing down the stone steps that led to the Thames police station. A moment later and he was kneeling beside Diana.

The girl looked pale and ill and her hair was still wet from her immersion in the river, but she had been well wrapped up in blankets and lay before a blazing fire in the charge-room.

'Jim!' she breathed, and looked up at him with shining eyes.

While he spoke to her, the melancholy sergeant had a word with Yarle with the result that three minutes after their arrival Jim had taken a hurried farewell of the girl, and found himself ensconced in the bowers of a fast police launch, and speeding up the river. The drizzle of rain had developed into a downpour as Sergeant Yarle ordered the boat to slow down and pointed to the bank.

'That's the place, sir,' he said shortly. 'It hasn't been occupied for two years.'

He had hardly finished speaking when

Jim saw a long black shape slip out of the shadows, and heard the rhythmic chug-chug of a high-powered motor.

'That's a launch!' he exclaimed sharply, 'and travelling without lights. I'll bet that's our man.'

The boat had reached the centre of the river and was gathering speed as Yarle barked an order. Jim had to grasp the side of the tiny shelter as the police boat swung round sharply and went racing off in pursuit. Peering through the mist of mingled spray and rain, he could just make out the vague shadow of the fleeing launch, a rapidly-moving smudge upon the dark surface of the water.

Sergeant Yarle shouted something to the man at the wheel of the police boat, and it quivered as it put on speed. Gradually they overtook the launch ahead, and slowly drew in alongside.

'We've got him now!' cried Yarle excitedly, and stopped as there came a swift stab of flame from the launch beside them.

A bullet buried itself with a thud in the

wooden shelter. *Crack!* A second bullet flew viciously past the side of Jim's head and he felt in his pocket for his own automatic. A veritable fusillade of shots followed, but fortunately they went wide, and in the momentary lull immediately after, Sergeant Yarle, accompanied by two men, succeeded in leaping from the police boat into the launch. Jim heard a snarled oath, and then a splash.

'He's in the river!' came Yarle's voice, and the man at the wheel of the police boat switched on a searchlight, and sent the ray dancing over the dark surface of the river.

Presently it picked up the black dot of a man's head. With long powerful strokes the swimmer was making for the opposite bank, Jim stripped off his coat and kicked off his shoes. Steadying himself for a second, he dived, and went off in pursuit of that bobbing black head. The other had had a good start, but he was hampered by the clothes he was wearing, for he had not had time even to discard his coat, and gradually Jim overlook him. When he was a yard away the fugitive turned, and in the light of the searchlight Jim saw his white, rage-distorted face. Treading water he stretched out his hand to grip 'The Big Fellow' by the collar, but the man dived, and coming up behind Jim flung an arm round his neck. They sank together, the young inspector fighting desperately to break the other's stranglehold, but he held on.

Jim's lungs were bursting, and there was a loud buzzing in his head, and then suddenly the other's grasp relaxed, and the young inspector shot to the surface, and drew in great gasping breaths of relief. He heard a shout near him, and looking round saw that Yarle had brought up the police boat.

'Have you got him, sir?' asked Yarle, peering over the side.

Jim shook his head.

'No,' he began breathlessly. 'We — '

'There he is, sir!' cried the man at the wheel, and they caught a momentary glimpse of a dark form, as it appeared for a second on the surface of the water. It came up close to the side of the police boat, and leaning over, Yarle succeeded in gripping the back of the coat. With the help of the man who came to his assistance they succeeded in dragging 'The Big Fellow' on board. A few moments later Jim himself scrambled over the side of the police boat, and looked shiveringly at the thing they had taken from the river.

'I don't think you'll have any more trouble with him, sir,' said Yarle, as they stared down at the motionless form. 'He must have hit his head on something at the bottom. Look!' He pointed to the gaping wound at the back of the man's skull, and Jim nodded.

Bending down he turned the dead man gently over, and looked at the white face. It was Leslie Venning!

⋆   ⋆   ⋆

'He was a clever man,' said Sergeant Wiles sadly, shaking his head. 'Pity he had a kink. You know when I come across people like that, it always makes me think what might have happened to me.'

'When you've finished your lecture on

philosophy,' said Jim, 'perhaps you'll do something useful. Those reports — '

'I'll see all about them,' said the sergeant. 'By the way Mr. Littleton rang up just before you came in and said he was coming along.'

Jim grunted disgustedly.

'I shan't be here,' he said. 'I've got an appointment. You can tell him all he wants to know.'

'He used to go to Venmng's flat, didn't he?' asked Wiles.

'Yes,' said Jim. 'Why?'

'I was thinking,' answered the sergeant slowly, 'that it was probably during one of his visits that he lost that button.'

'Does it matter?' asked the young inspector. 'We know Venning got hold of it in some way.'

'Yes; but I like to be tidy,' said Wiles. 'I don't like loose ends hanging about. When I was a boy — '

'I've no time to listen to reminiscences of your revolting childhood,' broke in Jim with a glance at his watch, and rising to his feet. 'I must go now, if anybody wants me tell them that I'm attending an important conference.'

'Remember me to the young lady, won't you?' said Wiles as he went out and shut the door.

The Man on the Train

(Edited and completed by Chris Verner)

In his large, comfortably furnished office, Michael Dene, *No 55*, of the British Intelligence Service, sat at his big flat-topped desk at the Foreign Office. His grey eyes looked thoughtfully at a file open in front of him marked *Red Fox* and stamped *Top Secret*. He had just received word that Red Fox was fleeing the country.

Red Fox was a German agent working at the Air Ministry, rumbled by Dene over a year ago. Rather than capture him and lock him up, Britain's Special Operations Executive, the covert World War II espionage agency created by Winston Churchill, deliberately fed him false information about British airfields to give a totally false impression of Britain's air defences. The British Intelligence Service knew it was only a matter of time before Red Fox discovered his cover had been blown and his true identity discovered.

Then he would know he was being used. That time had now arrived.

Michael Dene picked up the telephone.

'Is that Harlequin? This is Dene. Listen carefully . . . *Red Fox is running.* I repeat . . . *Red Fox is running . . .* '

He spoke on the secure line for nearly twenty minutes. When he had finished his call he hung up and immediately activated the intercom on his desk: 'I'll need a plane standing by at Northolt. Please see to it immediately.'

★　★　★

If Superintendent Robert Budd had caught the train he originally intended to catch, instead of arriving at the station in time to see the rear coach disappearing in the distance, he might never have become involved in the strange affair of the man on the train. But he did miss the train to Westpool, and had to wait for the next, a fact which caused him a great deal of irritation.

It was seldom that the big man took a

holiday away from his neat little villa in Streatham. Usually he was content to spend such periods of leisure as came his way in the garden among his beloved roses. But he had not been feeling too good lately; a long spell of hard work had brought on something akin to a breakdown and his doctor had insisted on a complete change of air.

'Go somewhere by the sea,' he said. 'Spend most of your time lying on the beach in the sun — if you're lucky enough to get any — at any rate get plenty of sea air and lots of sleep . . . '

Mr. Budd had protested. He did not care for the sea, he explained. He would rather be in his own garden. But the doctor was adamant. If his advice was ignored he wouldn't be held responsible for the big man's future health.

After a great deal of argument, Mr. Budd had reluctantly agreed to do as he was told. And now he had missed the train. The next, he discovered, did not go for two hours, and he cast about for some means of passing the time. Carrying a battered leather case, he made his way to

141

the buffet. It was early and the place held only a smattering of people.

He secured a cup of steaming coffee and a ham sandwich from the disinterested waitress behind the bar, took them over to a small marble-topped table, sat down, and surveyed the people around him through his heavy-lidded, sleepy-looking eyes. He wondered how many of the people in the buffet were waiting for the fast train to Westpool. He liked to guess at another person's story solely from observation.

This wasn't just an idle pastime, it was directly related to his job. The way they interacted, their body language, their leisure pursuits, their speech and conversation, even smell, provided an instant snapshot of a person — their motivation and life story. This first impression could be modified as new facts came to light. It was always interesting to see how supportive such facts were. A lot of his work was observation, attention to detail followed by speculation, and then backing up that speculation with facts.

There were not many very interesting

subjects for speculation in the buffet, until an elderly gentleman with a walking stick entered. He limped up to the counter and ordered a coffee. He looked to be over seventy with silvery grey hair and a badly trimmed moustache. He wore thick-rimmed spectacles. On the top of his head was a flat cap which was pulled down over his face. He was dressed in an ill-fitting black suit, and his shoes were scuffed with worn down heels. Mr. Budd thought he looked impoverished. Like his shoes, the old man looked worn down. The walking stick was of the cheap variety and, by contrast to the elderly gentleman's appearance, it looked new and shiny. Mr. Budd wondered what his story was and where he was going.

Perhaps he was on his way to visit a relation? Or had he been on a visit and was now on his way home? But he carried no overnight bag, or luggage of any kind. He paid for his coffee with a pocket full of loose change, carefully counting it out as if money was scarce, and carried his coffee into a far shady corner as far away from other people as possible where the lighting was dim — an intriguing character, thought the fat detective.

A well-dressed man in a dark suit and trilby strode in. Mr. Budd estimated he was in his late forties. He was swarthy-skinned with a slightly foreign appearance. Now, here was somebody completely different, thought Mr. Budd, looking through sleepy eyes at the man's shoes, a pair of polished brogues you could see your face in. Here was a confident and purposeful professional man.

The man marched up to the bar, and bought a packet of cigarettes. He turned with his back to the bar, surveying everyone in the buffet, as he leisurely took a cigarette out of the pack, lit it, and strode out again into the terminus.

Mr. Budd demolished his sandwich and took a long drink of the hot coffee. He looked at his watch. Still a short while to kill until the train arrived. The click clack of high heels made him look up.

A girl in her early thirties walked in. She was smartly dressed in a tweed suit and matching brown high heels, and carried an expensive handbag. Her long blonde hair fell about her shoulders in curls. She paused and looked round, aware that every eye in the room was watching her.

Mr. Budd recognised her immediately. He recalled that back at Scotland Yard there was a file full of facts on Tania Watts. He recalled she came from an old Deptford family, all of them crooks. Her upbringing hadn't encouraged her to aspire to much, other than continue in the family trade. He also remembered she had three brothers, one of them he knew, if not two, were residing at His Majesty's pleasure in Pentonville. Unlike the rest of her family Tania was smart. She concealed her roots carefully. She'd taken elocution lessons and sought work in several good hotels in order to observe and learn social skills. It hadn't taken her long to move into the West End of London and then a few years later graduate to a flat in Knightsbridge.

As she caught sight of him she gave him a mocking smile.

'Good morning, Superintendent,' she greeted.

Mr. Budd sighed.

Tania Watts was a vision of loveliness, there could be no denying that fact.

'Good morning to you, Miss Watts,' he answered, 'and what brings yer to this wondrous place at this particular hour?'

'Call me Tania,' answered the girl sweetly, avoiding answering the question. 'I could ask you the same thing?'

Mr. Budd grunted. 'If yer want to know, I'm on leave. I'm waiting to catch a train for Westpool.'

'Westpool!' The girl's eyebrows went up. 'That's a happy coincidence, Superintendent — or should I call you Mr. Budd . . . '

'Mr. Budd will do fine.' His sleepy eyes were watching her closely. 'I'm not sure happiness comes into it. Takin' your annual holiday I suppose?' he asked cynically.

Tania Watts gave him her mocking smile again and avoided any direct answer. 'A girl has to earn a living,' she said. 'May I sit down?'

Mr. Budd nodded. 'It's never too late ter mend your ways,' he suggested benevolently, finishing off his coffee, as Tania made herself comfortable.

'Are you on a case?' she asked, lowering her voice.

Mr. Budd smiled. 'I told yer, I'm on leave. I'm supposed to be resting — lying on the beach.'

The thought of Mr. Budd lying on a beach caused her to break into a fit of giggles.

'I'm sorry!' she apologised, her hand flying to her mouth. She looked at the big man seating opposite her, and burst into a fresh fit.

Mr. Budd surveyed her from half-closed lids. 'I can't see anything amusin',' he remarked, wondering what had got into her.

Tania took a handkerchief from her handbag and wiped her eyes.

'Oh, that was so funny!' she exclaimed, when she had composed herself.

'I'm glad I've managed to brighten up your day,' retorted the big man sarcastically. 'Can I get yer something to drink?'

'A cup of tea, please,' answered Tania.

Mr. Budd sighed again, as he heaved

his prodigious bulk off the chair and walked ponderously over to the bar. He tried to get the attention of the waitress who seemed intent on looking the other way.

'What if I told you I was turning over a new leaf . . . ' Tania said, when he'd returned and set down her tea and another steaming coffee for himself.

'If yer turned over a whole book it wouldn't make much difference,' retorted Mr. Budd unkindly. 'You've got used to living the easy way, Miss Watts. Easy come, easy go. I can't see you suddenly slaving away for a living like the rest of us . . . '

'I've done my share of slaving,' said Tania. 'I never intend to slave again!'

Mr. Budd nodded. 'I'm sure you don't,' he agreed.

'What if I told you I had sufficient money to live comfortably for the rest of my life?' she confided, her green eyes watching him, as she sipped her tea.

'I'd feel very sorry for the unfortunate men you've duped,' answered Mr. Budd unkindly. 'The promise you inspire in them is never attained, which seems unfair.'

A hard look came into her face for a second, as she put her cup down. 'Life is unfair, Mr. Budd.'

'More unfair for some than for others . . . I have to agree with that.' Mr. Budd was thinking she'd suffered a pretty tough childhood. He slowly rubbed his chin. 'In my many years as a policeman I have come to realise one true thing, Miss Watts: a leopard doesn't change its spots.'

Tania rolled her eyes and made a face. She was just about to reply to him when she was distracted by the elderly man with the stick, who had scraped back his chair noisily and appeared to be leaving. He began limping towards the entrance. Her eyes followed him as he pushed open the door and went out into the terminus.

Mr. Budd wondered what her interest was in the elderly man. He didn't look the type that would normally have occupied Tania's attention.

'If we want decent seats on the train it might be a good time to make a move,' she said, pushing her chair back.

Tania led Mr. Budd onto the platform and past the first few coaches of the waiting train. Ahead of them the elderly man had paused by an open door and, turning his head, was looking back at them. Then he climbed aboard and the door slammed shut.

Mr. Budd followed Tania because it would have been rude not to, and whilst he wasn't overjoyed to have Tania Watts as a travelling companion the alternative might be much worse. He followed her along the corridor until she paused outside a compartment and entered.

The compartment was unoccupied except for a corridor seat which was occupied by the elderly man with the walking stick. He was slumped in the corner and appeared to have fallen asleep.

Tania led Mr. Budd over to the window seats and sat down. Mr. Budd heaved his battered leather case up onto the rack noticing that Tania carried no luggage — there was no sign of a porter. He settled himself in comparative comfort opposite her, wondering for the second time what it was about the elderly gentleman with the walking stick that attracted her. It was obvious she had chosen the compartment because he was in it.

It struck Mr. Budd that fate had a cynical sense of humour to have arranged for him to sit opposite one of London's most successful con artists. She was a woman who had been a subject of attention at Scotland Yard since she had reached the age of eighteen. She was an expert liar and had never been prosecuted, which he considered was testimony to her artfulness. Mr. Budd had to admit to himself he had a sneaking admiration for her — a soft spot — until he considered how she had accumulated her money. If she'd chosen to become an actress, he had no doubts she would have made a very successful one. It was impossible to tell when Tania Watts was acting and when she wasn't.

'What are you going to do in Westpool?' she asked as they waited for the train to leave.

'As little as possible,' answered Mr. Budd truthfully.

A smart young man in an immaculate grey flannel suit entered the compartment and sat in the other corridor seat opposite the sleeping man, diagonally opposite Tania.

He opened a new, expensive-looking, pigskin briefcase and took out a book. Mr. Budd saw it was a cheap edition of a popular thriller. The young man studiously began to read it, but kept glancing up. He couldn't take his eyes off Tania. It obvious he was trying to avoid staring at her.

She didn't have to lift a finger, thought Mr. Budd resignedly; they came to her like moths to a flame, witless to the fact that beneath that beautiful exterior was a master criminal waiting to skin them alive. He thought of a Venus flytrap.

Mr. Budd had bought a magazine to while away the journey, but the stories and articles were not very good, and after a while he put it down on his knee and watched two of the ugliest girls he had ever seen enter the compartment and sit along from Tania. They were sufficiently alike for Mr. Budd to conclude they were sisters. They had short, curly, straw-coloured hair and wore bright red lipstick. They were followed by a much overdressed fat woman, who struggled into the compartment with a large suitcase. She had difficulty lifting her case onto the rack. It was a comic performance that reduced the ugly girls to giggles as they whispered spiteful remarks. Mr. Budd was about to go to her assistance, when the man in the dark suit and trilby entered — the man he had watched purchase cigarettes in the buffet.

The compartment was now full. People who had got on late were passing along the corridor anxiously looking for a seat.

The man in the Trilby deftly lifted the fat woman's heavy case, sliding it onto the rack.

'Thank you,' she said, breathing heavily. 'You are very kind.'

The man shook his head. 'Not at all, Madam,' he said, with a slight East London accent, as he removed his Trilby and placed it on the rack, exposing a head of dark wavy hair. He sat between her and the young man with the grey flannel suit, who produced a magazine from his inside pocket and proceeded to leaf through it.

Mr. Budd leaned forward and pretended to look at someone in the corridor, in order to see what the magazine was. He judged the man to be something in the engineering line, for he was reading a technical magazine devoted to turbine-engines. As he rapidly turned the pages, presumably looking for a particular article, Mr. Budd saw there were a great many graphs and mathematical calculations. The whole thing looked appallingly dull.

The fat lady wedged herself up against Mr. Budd as she glared at the ugly sisters with extreme displeasure. He hoped she wasn't about strike up a conversation.

He lifted up his magazine and pretended to be very interested in it.

There were several piercing whistles from somewhere down the platform. With a sudden jerking of the coaches, and an answering blast of a steam whistle, the train began slowly to pull out of the station.

Mr. Budd looked at his watch. The train was running five minutes late. He smiled at Tania, the only occupant of the compartment who wasn't a stranger, and watched the train gather speed as it slowly and heavily crabbed sideways across points that took it across the tracks to the main coastal line. Another train coming into the station went past, and for a moment the windows were obscured by clouds of steam.

He glanced across at Tania to find her looking at him suspiciously.

Mr. Budd assumed she thought his explanation that he was on leave and taking a holiday was an invention, and that he was on a case tracking down some criminal or other. He wondered if she had anything to hide, and if she did, why she was travelling with him.

The wheels of the train clicked monotonously as they rattled over the rails, creating a unique tempo beat, as it left the environs of London. It was soon speeding through a picturesque country-side of fields, woodland, roads, cuttings and stations . . . The day had started out sunny, but now the sky was a blanket of grey cloud. Mr. Budd wondered gloomily if it would start raining, and if it would continue to rain for his entire stay at Westpool.

Tania leaned forward and tapped him on his knee. 'Is there a restaurant car?' she asked brightly.

Mr. Budd shook his head.

'I was told there wasn't,' he answered, 'which is a pity.'

'It always breaks up the journey if you can go to a restaurant car,' she said, smiling.

Mr. Budd agreed.

But there was no restaurant car and, after half an hour, Mr. Budd began to feel cramped and desperate for one of his rank, black cigars. He heaved himself up, murmured an excuse, opened the compartment door, and stepped into the corridor, which was thankfully deserted. He slid open a window.

A few seconds later he was smoking contentedly.

From where he stood he could see into the next compartment. It contained a family: mother, father, three children and a grandmother. The children were over-excited and obviously couldn't wait to get to their holiday destination. They were jumping up and down and shouting, forcing their parents to keep up an endless volley of *sit down, be quiet*, and *keep still*, all to no avail. There were two spare seats which Mr. Budd noted no one seemed to have taken. He fully understood why.

Suddenly with no warning, a long goods train shot by, travelling towards London, buffeting the air between the two trains, and jolting Mr. Budd so severely he had to grab the brass handrail. It gave him a momentary shock. He felt like he was being attacked by an invisible force. Just as he recovered his balance, there was a piercing scream from the whistle, and the train suddenly plunged into a tunnel. The lights didn't come on and everything went dark. The children in the family compartment screamed, and then burst out laughing, as they got overexcited, inventing ways to frighten one another.

It was a short tunnel and the train was soon in the open again, speeding through a cutting covered in primroses. Some spots of rain smacked against the windows and streaked diagonally across the glass.

Mr. Budd reflected he would be getting a lot more relaxation if he'd been at home in his garden. He imagined it was still sunny there. He thought of brewing a nice pot of tea, sitting at his little garden table in the shade, and breathing in the scent of his roses. No sooner had this thought crossed his mind than the train plunged into another tunnel, and a damp foul smell entered the open window right next to him. Still the lights didn't come on. It was noisy as hell and dark as pitch. He watched with little comfort the end of his cigar glowing in the dark, while he listened to the renewed screams of the children in the compartment behind him, as they renewed attempts to scare the wits out of each other.

As he was realising this tunnel was much longer than the last one, and wondering just how long, there was a sudden momentary flash of light. A bright spark that showed up the corridor in stark relief, before plunging it into darkness once again. So short lived was it, that he thought he might have imagined it. He wondered what had caused it.

Working through several possibilities he deduced it had probably been caused by someone striking a flint — a flint sparking momentarily from the wheel of a lighter?

Then someone in a hurry crashed into him, pushing him forward against the window, so that his cigar, striking the glass in a shower of sparks, was knocked from his fingers.

Through the noise of the train and the screams of the children, he heard something metallic clatter to the floor. Mr. Budd could see nothing in the inky blackness, as he struggled to regain his balance, now winded, and in a thoroughly bad mood, he wondered why he had been so foolish to have listened to his doctor.

A few seconds later a faint grey light appeared at the windows and, very soon after, the train ran out of the tunnel into a cutting of long shadows and bright sunlight.

Blinking a little at the sudden transition from darkness to light, Mr. Budd looked down at the floor of the corridor. At first he failed to see what it was that he had heard fall, and then he saw it. It lay about two yards away, close up against the outer wall of the coach. It was a long-bladed knife and the blade was smeared with fresh blood!

Mr. Budd stared at the sinister object, unable to believe the evidence of his own eyesight. But there was no doubt the knife was really there. He took out his handkerchief, went over to it and, holding onto the handrail for support, bent down and carefully picked it up between two podgy fingers.

The thin blade was about six inches long and looked razor sharp. It was set in a steel handle, and the whole of its length bore traces of fresh blood.

The big man's eyes almost closed as he surveyed the grim weapon, but all sleepiness had left them and he was totally alert.

Whose blood stained the sharp steel? What had happened on that train as it tore through the darkness of the tunnel? Obviously the person who had bumped into him had dropped the knife. He wrapped it carefully in his handkerchief and slipped it into his pocket.

He groaned inwardly, as he was forced to acknowledge that somewhere on the train someone might be wounded and he should make a search without delay.

A scream, shrill and full of horror, made him swing round. The door of his compartment was open, and staggering through it was the fat woman in disarray. She crashed into the corridor window waving her arms wildly, lost her balance, and almost fell over. Her flabby face was the colour of chalk under the layer of make-up, so that the rouge stood out in startling contrast. She looked clownish, but there was nothing funny about the stark terror that filled her eyes.

'Get someone!' she screamed at Mr. Budd. 'He's been killed . . . He's dead! Murdered!'

'Who's dead, Madam?' he asked in a

deliberately calm voice designed to dampen her hysteria. He took a step towards her.

With a stubby finger glittering with rings, the fat woman stabbed towards the open door behind her. She had difficulty breathing.

'That nice man next to me,' she blurted out.

Mr. Budd reached the compartment just as Tania Watts stepped out of it; she was as white as a sheet, her eyes wide and desperate.

'There's been some trouble,' she told Mr. Budd. 'A man's been attacked — seriously attacked — a lot of blood! I think it could be fatal!'

'You stay out here,' instructed Mr. Budd. 'I'll take a look.'

'It was very sudden in the dark — a flash of light, an arm . . . ' Tania was saying, as Mr. Budd pushed past her and stepped adroitly into the compartment.

The first thing the stout man noticed was the technical magazine the man in the Trilby had been reading, trodden on, and torn, on the floor at the feet of the two ugly sisters. The sisters sat very still and very shocked, staring at the man in front of them, slumped forward, with a knife wound clearly visible in his throat.

The knife had entered the neck just under the right ear, a deep stab that appeared, from the amount of blood, as though it had severed an artery. Mr. Budd felt his pulse — there was none, confirming the man was dead.

Next to the dead man, pressed into the corner sat the man in the grey suit, fingering his cheek with an expression of complete incredulity.

Blood flecked the side of his face, was spattered over his suit, and across the white pages of the thriller lying open on his lap.

There was no sign of the old man who had been asleep opposite, or his walking stick.

Mr. Budd realised it was important to find a doctor as soon as possible and get help. He stepped back into the corridor wondering how he was going to achieve this.

Tania was sympathising with the fat

woman who looked in a terrible state. 'You have absolutely no idea what happened?' he asked Tania, interrupting.

She looked at him, wide-eyed. 'I could feel a commotion and hear scuffling, but I couldn't see anything properly,' Tania answered. 'Someone stabbed him, didn't they?' Seeing the suspicious look in Mr. Budd's eye, she added, 'I promise you, on my mother's grave, this had nothing to do with me!'

Mr. Budd wanted to believe her. She may be one of London's smartest con women, but he didn't think she was capable of murder. But that didn't completely rule out the possibility she had something to do with it, though he couldn't put his finger on what it might be.

The murdered man had been the last to enter the compartment. That was very odd, Mr. Budd thought. Very odd indeed, if it had been a premeditated crime, because how did the murderer already sitting there, know his victim would enter the compartment? The murdered man was the last one into the compartment.

He might have chosen to sit somewhere else, even another coach . . .

'Nobody is accusing anyone of anything,' he assured her. 'Was there an argument? Did you hear any raised voices?'

'Nothing like that,' she replied, pointing with alarm to the empty corridor seat. 'Where's the old man gone?'

Mr. Budd rubbed his chin gently as he surveyed the empty seat. It was a question he was asking himself.

He saw in his mind the old man spring up out of his seat, flick a lighter to create a spark, enough to locate his victim in the dark, stab him, and then flee into the corridor, where in the dark he had bumped into him, dropped the knife, and ran off . . . Where? There was nowhere to run to. He was trapped on a moving train.

'I'll go and fetch the guard,' said Tania.

Mr. Budd had just been thinking of asking her to do exactly that. He nodded. 'That would be very helpful.'

She gave him a quick, grateful look, for entrusting her with this task, and rushed off towards the rear of the train.

165

Mr. Budd turned to the fat woman who was clinging onto the rail and gulping in air from the open window like a landed fish. She looked as if she would be sick at any moment.

'I don't think there's anywhere else to sit,' he told her. 'Except in there . . . ' He indicated the compartment with the family and their obstreperous children.

'I'm alright here,' she answered, unable to resist a glance through the window at the dead man. 'I can't go back in there!'

Mr. Budd's attention swung back to the compartment, to the two ugly girls who looked frozen in time, like waxwork dummies, the man in the grey suit, and the dead man.

'I'm a perlice officer and I will be taking charge 'ere until we can get outside help,' he told them. 'We've sent for the guard. Obviously, you are witnesses to a serious incident.' He pointed to the empty corridor seat. 'Do any of yer know what happened to the elderly gentleman who was sitting there?'

They shook their heads.

No one knew what had happened to

him. The general consensus of opinion was that he had been there asleep before the train entered the long tunnel and was gone by the time it came out. Not very helpful.

Mr. Budd turned his head sleepily from the murdered man to the empty seat. A murder and a vanishing!

Not a good start to his holiday!

Not at all relaxing!

What next? A derailment?

He sighed, as he produced a notebook, which he always carried with him, from his inside pocket.

'We'd better start with yer names,' he said, backing into the corridor until he was facing the fat woman who was still hanging onto the guard rail. She didn't look well and was still breathing erratically.

'Now, Madam,' he addressed the fat woman. 'What's yer name?'

'Mrs. Maltby-Danvers,' she replied.

Mr. Budd wrote the name down in his notebook. 'Maltby . . . '

'Maltby-Danvers, with a hyphen,' she said.

'Maltby-Danvers, with a hyphen,' he repeated slowly as he wrote. 'Can you tell me what happened?'

'There was flash, and I saw . . . I saw the outline of a man leaning towards me. His eyes were wild . . . His arm was raised . . . That's all I saw. That poor man next to me!' she gasped and blinked. 'Right next to me . . . '

'Yes, I saw that flash,' said Mr. Budd. 'You're sure it was a man?'

'Of course I'm sure! I'll never forget those cold eyes as long as I live.'

Mr. Budd nodded sympathetically. 'Was it the elderly gentleman?'

'There was nothing elderly about him,' retorted Mrs. Maltby-Danvers.

'Did he have white hair?' asked Mr. Budd, remembering clearly the elderly gentleman in the cap with his white hair sticking out.

'I think so . . . '

'It was a lighter?' asked the big man.

Mrs. Maltby-Danvers nodded. 'I could hear the wheel against a flint . . . it's an unmistakable sound . . . Then that spark!'

The detective nodded. 'He needed to

see what he was doing.'

'He looked like a vicious beast!' Her hand went to her heart as she gulped in air. 'Like a photograph of a wild animal.'

'Was he wearing a cap?'

'I only remember his eyes . . . Oh, yes . . . I remember now, I saw his moustache.'

That settled it, thought the detective. 'It had to have been the man sitting opposite?'

'Of course it was!' she exclaimed, peering at the empty seat. 'He's gone, hasn't he?'

Mr. Budd had to agree that it looked conclusive the elderly man was responsible for the attack, and then fled.

'Did you notice anything else?' he asked. 'Anything at all . . . ?'

Mrs. Maltby-Danvers looked trapped. 'Obviously a commotion, then a kind of gasp . . . I heard the sound of paper tearing . . . his magazine I think, and a kind of snort . . . It was like somebody had fallen asleep . . . There was a lot of screaming from the next compartment — those noisy children . . . '

'Did you hear the door open?'

'No,' she answered. 'You left it open when you went out for a smoke.'

Mr. Budd noted that the door to the corridor had been open for the entire sequence of events. He thanked her, and turned his attention to the three remaining occupants of the compartment.

He took their names and questioned them one by one. He learned that the man in the dapper grey suit was Geoffrey Purvis, and that he lived in Westpool. He was something to do with a hotel chain.

'What do you remember?' asked Mr. Budd.

Geoffrey Purvis spoke in a thin nasal voice that was at odds with his dapper appearance: 'I saw a flash, a man standing in front of me with a lighter — it was so quick, then it was dark again.' He'd felt a bump against his leg, and then felt a struggle, then splashes against his cheek.

'Anything else?' prompted Mr. Budd.

'I'm pretty certain it was the old man opposite.' Geoffrey Purvis thought hard for a moment trying to remember. 'I heard the sound of tearing paper,' he said.

'That was the loudest thing I heard, after the lighter — tearing and bunching up of paper crunched underfoot.'

Mr. Budd grunted. This wasn't going to get him very far. 'I suggest we all move out into the corridor,' he said, pulling down the blinds. 'Leave your luggage; I'll make sure it's safe.'

He looked at the torn and flattened engineering magazine at their feet and, surprisingly quickly for a man of his bulk, picked up what was left of it. It was dirty and covered in bloody footprints. He picked it up and put on top of his case.

Once out in the corridor, he learned that the two ugly sisters' names were Beatrice and Elizabeth Rice. They were travelling from London to stay with their aunt in Westpool for a short holiday. Beatrice had been the one sitting next to the old man.

Mr. Budd asked her: 'Did the man next to you move at all during the time the compartment was in darkness?'

Beatrice looked at her sister for support, as if they had an unwritten agreement that one couldn't speak without the permission of the other. 'I heard a springy sound and felt the seat move. That was when he must have got up.'

'It was all very sudden,' added Elizabeth.

'I felt him brush my thigh,' Beatrice added, her eyes opening wide. 'Then something knocked my arm.'

'There was a commotion?' asked Mr. Budd.

'We both sensed that,' answered Elizabeth, looking at her sister, 'didn't we Beatty?'

Beatrice nodded. 'Yes we did, and we heard footsteps as he ran out.'

'There was a lot of commotion,' Elizabeth confirmed. 'We heard the paper tearing and crunching too . . . '

'That was the dead gentleman's magazine, wasn't it?' asked Beatrice.

They had all heard the sound Mrs. Maltby-Danvers had described. It was the sort of sound that a person makes when they catch their breath. The big man had no doubt that was exactly what it had been — the last quick breath of a dying man as the knife had struck. For death would have been instantaneous.

There would have been no time for a cry — nothing other than that sharp sound they had all heard *like someone snorting in their sleep*.

The two sisters went into the next compartment and occupied the two vacant seats next to the children. They became instantly the focus of attention as everyone began talking at once, desperate to find out what had been happening.

A man in the uniform of a Railway Guard arrived looking agitated.

'What's happened, sir?' he asked Mr. Budd.

Mr. Budd told him who he was, and asked the guard's name.

'Gregory Thompson, sir,' the guard answered.

The guard looked into the compartment and noticed the lifeless form on the seat. 'My Lord! Is 'e . . . ?'

'I'm afraid he is quite dead,' cut in Mr. Budd.

The guard shook his head in disbelief.

'I've never seen anything like that before . . . '

'I hope you never do again,' retorted Mr. Budd.

'Shall I stop the train?' asked the guard.

'I don't think that'll serve any great purpose,' said Mr. Budd, looking out of the window at the passing countryside.

'Stopping the train will leave us stranded in the middle of nowhere. Send a telegram at once to Westpool perlice. Tell 'em there's been a murder and ask them to meet the train. No one must get off this train until all are accounted for, and statements taken.'

'Right you are, sir,' acknowledged the guard.

'Now, Mr. Thompson, I want you to send that telegram as a matter of utmost priority, but keep yer eyes open for an elderly gentleman with a walking stick. If you see 'im be very careful . . . do not try to speak to 'im, or approach 'im in any way. You understand?'

'Yes, sir,' answered the guard.

'Do nothing to attract his attention, you understand?' emphasised the big man. 'If you do see 'im come and fetch me immediately.'

'Who is he?' asked the guard, his ferret face contorting with curiosity.

'I wish I knew,' answered Mr. Budd, rubbing his chin. 'He was sitting there.' He indicated the empty seat. 'During the attack on the victim he disappeared. It is reasonable to assume he was the attacker, and he's somewhere on this train.' He watched the guard through half-closed eyelids. 'He could be a very dangerous man.'

'Right you are, sir.' The guard touched his cap. 'I'll keep a look out for him.'

'Thank you.

The guard frowned for a moment. 'The elderly gentleman murdered . . . ' He tilted his head towards the dead man in the compartment

Mr. Budd sighed. 'I have no firm idea at the moment, Mr. Thompson,' he grunted wearily, thinking of his roses, 'but it certainly looks that way. When you've sent the telegram come back here, please.'

Shortly after the guard had gone, Tania returned.

'Thank you for fetching the guard. That was very helpful, Miss Watts.'

'Tania,' she corrected. 'I told you, I've turned over a new leaf.'

Mr. Budd looked at her. What a picture she was, like one of his roses in full bloom. 'Maybe you have,' he acceded, watching her in admiration through half-closed eyelids. 'On the other hand, maybe you haven't.'

Geoffrey Purvis pushed past. 'I need to wash my face,' he mumbled, in his thin nasal voice, and set off in search of a wash basin.

'He's going to need a new suit,' commented Tania, wrinkling her nose at the sight of the blood spatter. 'This is very bad, isn't it?'

'All murder is,' retorted Mr. Budd.

'I suppose you've seen a lot of it?' asked Tania.

The big man nodded slowly. 'More than I would wish.'

The train went rushing on through the sunlit countryside as Mr. Budd began a careful search of the dead man's pockets . . .

He found a wallet with fifty pounds in five pound notes, and several identical cards that read *Peter Driscol, Structural Engineer*, followed by a number of abbreviated qualifications. There was an address in London. His pockets contained some keys, loose change. He recovered the magazine he'd put on top of his case and placed it on the seat. Then he lifted his case down and put it carefully on the seat. Then he took from his pocket his keys, selected a small one, and opened the case. He placed the knife he had picked up, Pierre Driscol's keys, his wallet, and the battered magazine inside. Then he relocked it and replaced it on the overhead rack.

'I wonder why he was suddenly attacked like that?' Tania asked.

'Unprovoked?'

Mr. Budd pinched the loose flesh of his chin between a fat thumb and finger. 'We don't know it was unprovoked, do we, Miss Watts. But I agree, on the surface a seemingly motiveless crime, one stranger attacking another . . . '

'Maybe they weren't strangers?' suggested Tania.

Mr. Budd shrugged. 'It looks to me to be a crime of opportunity, a dark tunnel . . . a sudden impulse . . . '

'The elderly gentleman doesn't seem so elderly any longer . . . ' she commented, staring at him.

Geoffrey Purvis returned. He had removed all blood splatter from his face and had tried to clean up his clothing with little success other than to create a number of large damp patches with dark red centres.

Tania stated that she would go to the front of the train, then work her way back, looking for the missing man. Mr. Budd gave her the same advice he had given the guard about the dangers of approaching a possibly dangerous man.

When Tania had left, Mr. Budd began an interrogation of all the people in the coach, but none of them could tell him anything. They all affirmed vehemently that they had not left their seats during the time the train was in the tunnel. There was no sign of the elderly gentleman who had occupied the corridor seat; he seemed to have vanished into thin air.

Without having added one iota to his knowledge concerning the dead man, Mr. Budd felt frustrated and exhausted. He wondered why the guard had not returned. He should have sent the telegram by now and returned as instructed. He glanced at his watch. They would be arriving at Westpool in about fifteen minutes. The murderer must still be on the train and he mustn't be allowed to get off.

Tania Watts, Mrs. Maltby-Danvers, and Geoffrey Purvis had congregated at the far end of the corridor as far away from the compartment containing the dead man as possible. Mr. Budd went up to them and checked that they were all right. Then he made his way to the rear of the train to the guard's van to find the cause of the guard's delay. When he reached it the door was fastened.

Mr. Budd rapped upon the door with his fist and announced his presence.

With nerves and muscles braced the stout superintendent waited. He didn't know what to expect. He heard a bolt withdrawn and the door opened immediately, revealing the guard, who looked surprised to see the big man.

'Oh, it's you, sir,' he said. 'Can I help you?'

'You could have helped me by returning after you'd sent that telegram, like I asked,' grunted Mr. Budd, as he took a step forward into the guard's van.

The guard stepped back to make room.

'I got delayed,' said the guard apologetically.

Mr. Budd glanced at his notebook. 'Mr. Gregory Thompson, wasn't it?' he asked.

'That's right, sir.'

Mr. Budd surveyed the guard through half-closed lids. The man seemed on edge . . . The detective looked over to the telegraph desk. 'Did you get a reply?'

'Reply, sir?' The guard looked at him strangely.

'A reply to the telegram,' said Mr. Budd impatiently. 'The Westpool perlice.'

'No, sir.'

Mr. Budd looked into guard's steel-blue eyes. They were cold and hard, and in that moment he realised . . .

He staggered back, clapping a podgy hand to his forehead feigning illness.

'Are you all right, sir?' asked the guard.

Mr. Budd gasped for breath and staggering over to a bench seat, collapsed on it. 'I 'aven't been very well . . . ' he mumbled, clutching his capacious stomach, 'that's why I'm on the train.' He sunk his head and coughed a few times. 'I'm supposed ter take a rest in Westpool you see . . . ,' he spluttered.

Pretending to be in a state of collapse he was alert to everything going on around him. He noticed some spots of blood on the floor that had been partially rubbed out — evidence of the fate of the real guard . . .

Of course, the telegram hadn't been sent. There would be no police waiting for the train at Westpool.

Mr. Budd had noticed two tiny red sore marks on the guard's lip and a single wisp of silver hair, enough to tell him a fake moustache had been torn off in a hurry.

Keeping his eyes almost closed, he

looked from side to side, sweeping the interior, searching for any sign of a walking stick, or what might have been the fate of the real guard. Seeing nothing helpful he produced another coughing fit and as he cautiously looked up . . .

That was when a fist like a block of steel hit him in the face.

His head snapped back and hit the wooden wall of the van. He would have been knocked unconscious if the wood hadn't yielded, absorbing some of the force behind the blow.

He saw blackness and stars.

He could feel blood trickling down his face.

The side door of the guard's van opened with a bang, and the air, and the noise of the wheels on the rails, rushed in menacingly.

Mr. Budd knew the game was up. It was clear to him he was about to share the same fate as the real guard. He was no match for the strength of this man. While he struggled to think of a solution to his predicament he pretended to be semi-conscious.

But his delaying tactics didn't work.

He felt his arm grabbed in a vice-like grip.

He spluttered and coughed, letting his body go limp, as the grip tightened. He tensed his muscles, ready to launch himself at the man who held him.

Then his arm was almost wrenched out of its socket.

As the man pulled, Mr. Budd suddenly ceased resisting and went with him, throwing all his weight against the man.

The man let go, trying to get his balance, as they both crashed headlong into the cast iron stove. The bogus guard cursed in German as Mr. Budd slammed him into it. His cap fell off revealing light brown hair.

Bolted to the floor, the stove didn't yield at all.

Both men grunted in pain as they fought to recover.

Breathing heavily, the perspiration streaming down his fat cheeks, Mr. Budd uttered a little grunt of satisfaction as he stepped back, bought his arm round, and with all his weight behind it, struck the man a blow on the side of his head.

The German slid sideways, falling to the floor. He rolled over, away from Mr. Budd, clutching his head. Then he staggered to his feet. Taking advantage of the big man's lack of breath he went for his beefy arm again and this time swung Mr. Budd's bulk towards the open side of the van.

Mr. Budd crashed into the door heavily and desperately grabbed onto a metal bar. A horrible pain shot up his spine. He glimpsed houses flashing by and sidings with goods trains . . .

It felt they were approaching a terminus.

He could smell the sea air.

The German was striding towards him, his fists clenched, and his eyes totally without mercy.

Mr. Budd took a deep breath and summoned his last reserves of energy to defend himself.

'Keep very still and don't make a move!' It was the voice of Tania Watts, and there was no doubting she meant what she said.

Mr. Budd blinked with astonishment.

Tania Watts stood in the entrance to the guard's van holding an automatic in her hand and it was pointed at Mr. Budd!

The German stopped in his tracks and stared at her.

'Who are you?'

'I'm with Gunter,' she said, waving the barrel of the automatic towards the bench. 'You pig, sit down!' she ordered, addressing the detective in a harsh voice.

Mr. Budd fingered his bruised face and looked at her coldly as he moved slowly towards the bench, in obvious pain, and sat down as he was instructed.

'A leopard doesn't change its spots,' he growled, glaring at Tania.

'Shut up!' she ordered, taking a pair of handcuffs from her handbag. 'Take off your jacket.'

The German realised what she was doing and hurriedly took off his railway guard's jacket and threw it on the floor.

Beyond some trees Mr. Budd caught a glimpse of the sea through the open door of the guard's van. He needed to delay . . . delay . . .

'I'm getting too old for this sort of thing,' he grunted, holding his head and groaning. 'I'm supposed to be resting . . .'

Tania's face was a mask of evil. 'Take off your jacket now, or I'll shoot you in the leg!'

The detective slowly took off his jacket emptying his pockets as he did so.

The German tore the jacket from him and threw the contents of the pockets on the floor. A box of matches, a packet of black cigars, a notebook, a wallet, some keys . . .

Tania threw the German some handcuffs. 'Be quick!' she urged, indicating for him to handcuff the detective. He snapped the bracelets on Mr. Budd's thick wrists with a sneer, then put on Mr. Budd's jacket that was far too big for him.

'There is no time to lose!' cried Tania. 'We'll arrive any time now! The station will be crawling with Secret Service agents.' She waved the German towards the opening. 'The train has slowed down; you'll have to jump off. Your friends are waiting.'

The German eyed her suspiciously.

'How do I . . . ?'

'Red Fox go now! Be quick!'

The German darted behind the pipe from the stove and returned with the walking stick. He strode over to the open doorway and looked down at the track, calculating the train's speed. Then he looked first at Tania and then at Mr. Budd.

'Kill him!' he ordered.

He threw out the walking stick and jumped after it.

The moment the German disappeared from sight Tania dropped the gun. She rushed over to Mr. Budd. 'I'm so very sorry about that,' she said apologetically, her face full of concern as she unlocked the handcuffs.

'Are you all right?'

Mr. Budd stared at her in bewilderment.

'Of course I'm not all right!' he grunted irritably.

Tania looked at his eye sympathetically. 'That's a real shiner you're going to get there!'

'That makes me feel a lot better!'

'It was very important for him to get away, you see?' she explained.

'I don't see nothin',' responded the big man, rubbing his wrists. 'What the hell is going on? Who is this Red Fox feller?'

'He's a German spy.'

'Of course he is,' retorted Mr. Budd sarcastically. 'I should have known! Where's he gone?'

'If we're right, he's escaping by sea to France, then back to Germany.'

Mr. Budd rubbed his sore back. He was all bruises. 'If who's right?'

Tania brushed the question aside. 'I'm worried about you. Your poor face!'

'Who's the dead man?' asked the detective.

Tania hesitated, and then made up her mind to tell him the truth. 'Pierre is . . . was one of our agents. Red Fox must have suspected he was being tailed by him, and took his opportunity to strike when we entered the tunnel, when everything went black . . . We've lost a good agent,' she said sadly.

The fat detective shook his aching head

slowly. 'I suppose you're not making all of this stuff up?' he asked sceptically.

Tania forced a smile. 'You'll find out shortly. We'll be arriving at Westpool very soon now.'

Mr. Budd moved as if to stand up and winced. 'Of course the telegram was never sent.'

'I sent one,' said Tania.

'To the perlice?' asked the Superintendent in surprise, bending down painfully to gather up his belongings.

'No, to the Foreign Office,' answered Tania, giving him a helping hand.

'You work for the Foreign Office?' Mr. Budd cut in, unable to hide his astonishment. 'The world is all upside down, Miss Watts.'

'Not so upside down as it's going to be,' predicted Tania, shaking her head reproachfully. 'I told you I'd turned over a new leaf.'

*   *   *

As the train pulled into the station Mr. Budd could see a number of uniformed police constables spaced out along the platform. There were also two men in black suits and Trilbys who looked like replicas of the murdered man, Pierre Driscol. Once the train had stopped Tania hurried up to them and engaged in urgent conversation. Then she hurried off towards the platform barrier looking worried.

All along the train, doors were opening. People were already attempting to get off, dragging luggage, buckets and spades, and all kinds of paraphernalia. The constables instructed them to remain on board.

Mr. Budd groaned with pain as he slowly climbed down onto the platform with his battered case. He put it down and lit one of his evil-smelling black cigars. He took a long pull at it and blew a cloud of smoke, watching it rise up unfurling in the sunlight. He felt worn out but better.

The stationmaster was making a dramatic announcement which was distorted and echoed so much from platform to platform it was almost unintelligible:

'Passengers who have just arrived on the London to Westpool train, please stay on the train! Return to your seats . . . '

Mr. Budd walked ponderously towards two senior-looking policemen.

'I'm a police officer, Superintendent Robert Budd, of Scotland Yard. There's been a murder . . . two murders if I'm not mistaken, a passenger and a railway guard.' He showed them his identification.

They introduced themselves as Detective Inspector Quirrol and Sergeant Jepson. Quirrol was tall and fit-looking, his face tanned, with dark hair that was combed back. Jepson was shorter and fatter, with coarse sandy hair and pasty features. He didn't look as if he got out in the sun much. They had brought with them six constables and the divisional surgeon who, after a brief examination of the body, confirmed what Mr. Budd already knew — the man had been murdered by a knife wound to the throat.

Photographs were taken. The dead man's belongings were sent to be tested for fingerprints. Passengers were brought from the train onto the platform one by one or in small groups, and allowed to go to their various destinations after providing proof of identity and an address. Most of the passengers were holiday visitors to Westpool and gave both their permanent and a temporary holiday address, and lodging houses and hotels they were booked into.

Mr. Budd told the police officers what he had witnessed. Detective Inspector Quirrol listened with respect to the sleepy-eyed Superintendent's detailed account of what had happened, while Sergeant Jepson wrote it all down. It was not often they enjoyed the presence of a Scotland Yard man as a key witness to a murder.

Mr. Budd placed his battered case on a bench, opened it, and handed over the evidence he had collected the knife he had found in the corridor, still wrapped in his handkerchief, what was left of the magazine, and Pierre Driscol's keys and wallet. He opened the wallet showing them the small pack of calling cards.

'Pierre Driscol, Structural Engineer?' read

Quirrol. 'We'll have to trace him . . . '

'No need for that,' said a commanding voice. 'Pierre was working for us.'

Mr. Budd turned to see a distinguished, lean-faced man with a high forehead and keen, grey eyes. He could see that beneath a suit that bore the obvious cut of Savile Row was a strong muscular form. He recognized the man immediately. It was Michael Dene, the cleverest man in the British Secret Service and the head of the Special Branch.

Dene shook hands with Mr. Budd. 'Hello Superintendent,' he greeted.

'Who are you, sir?' demanded Quirrol, unable to hide his irritation at so many officials intruding upon his territory.

'I'm Michael Dene.'

'You're the man in charge of the harbour operation?' asked Quirrol.

'That is correct,' answered Dene. He looked round to make sure no one else was in earshot. 'This is a clandestine operation under need-to-know restrictions,' he warned, showing Detective Inspector Quirrol his identification. 'The truth should go no further than the four of us standing here and of course my agents. There is to be no investigation, no files of any kind . . . we're slapping a D notice on this incident, preventing the press from publishing any information which might be of use to a future enemy.'

'I see sir,' answered Quirrol. 'But with respect, this is a murder enquiry.'

'We know all about the man who was murdered and the man who murdered him and the railway guard. The case is closed, Detective Inspector. We expect to catch this chap very shortly,' Dene went on. 'He's a German agent who goes by the name of *Red Fox*. He is trying to escape back to Germany.'

'Red Fox?' queried the Detective Inspector.

Michael Dean's eyes gleamed. 'His real name is of no consequence. We have deliberately let him escape from the train so he will lead us to others who are assisting him. We are pretty certain there's a boat waiting to take him to France. The more we round up the better.'

'Let me get this straight, sir,' said Quirrol, scratching his head. 'This German agent, this Red Fox, as you call 'im, murdered the man in the train compartment? And murdered the man called Pierre Driscol, who worked for you?'

'Yes, that is correct,' confirmed Dene. 'He obviously thought if he got rid of Driscol, and then pretended to be a railway guard, he'd managed to fool us and get away. He very nearly did.' He turned to the big man. 'We owe you a debt of gratitude, Superintendent. Now you can enjoy your holiday.'

Mr. Budd nodded. 'Yes, and I know where I'm going to be spending it.' He turned and collared the stationmaster who was walking by. 'Stationmaster, when is the next train back to London!'

★ ★ ★

A few weeks later, Superintendent Robert Budd received an invitation from Michael Dene inviting him to dinner at his home in Pimlico.

The door was opened by his housekeeper, who introduced herself as Mrs. Maltby. She was a homely woman and gave the stout man a friendly smile of welcome.

'Ah, Superintendent Budd, we've been expecting you.'

She showed him into a pleasantly furnished drawing room.

Michael Dene was standing by the fireplace smoking a pipe when the stout man entered. 'I hope you're recovering, Superintendent?' he greeted, stepping forward and shaking his hand with a firm grip.

'From my holiday, you mean?' the big man answered, unable to hide a trace of sarcasm in his voice. 'Yes, I feel much better now.'

Dene looked at him closely, much to Mr. Budd's discomfort. 'I see you still have traces of facial trauma.'

'You should have seen me after I got home,' grunted the detective. 'My eye closed and the side of my face went black.'

Dene nodded sympathetically as he put down his pipe on a brass rack containing several others. 'I wanted to thank you properly, Superintendent, for your support in capturing the German agent known as Red Fox. Of course that's not his real name. His real name is Kurt Waldburg, he's known here as David Taylor. He'd managed to worm his way into the Air Ministry.'

Mr. Budd rubbed a large hand over his chin. 'I can see why you want to keep this under wraps, sir. You got 'im then?'

Dene nodded. 'Eventually . . . We had men watching the harbour. He led us to a boat moored up there called *Marissa*. We let him board it and then our agents closed in. We arrested him, together with two French agents, who were working for the Germans. We also found some papers, a map showing a secret route through France to German borders, and a code book — a very useful catch.'

'Did you recover the walking stick?' asked Mr. Budd.

Michael Dene gave him a curious look. 'The walking stick?' he repeated evasively.

Mr. Budd smiled. 'There must 'ave been something mighty important about that walking stick, the way he hid it so carefully behind the stove pipe, and then deliberately tossed it out the guard's van before 'e jumped off the train. Got me thinking . . . '

Dene nodded. 'Very good, Superintendent . . . I'm pleased to say we recovered the walking stick!'

'What was significant about it?' Mr. Budd persisted.

'The ferrule unscrews, revealing a hollow centre. Red Fox had hidden microfilm of some *real* aviation secrets in that walking stick. As you can imagine, it was vital we got the microfilm back before it was handed over to the Germans.'

'Yes, I can see that,' answered Mr. Budd, stroking his chin.

'Two days later we captured the prize, the man who controlled Red Fox. A top German agent called Gunter Heim.'

Mrs. Maltby knocked and entered the room carrying a paper carrier bag. She went up to Mr. Budd and handed the bag to him with a warm smile and a gleam in her eye. 'Your jacket, sir . . . All cleaned and pressed.'

'Thank you, Mrs. Maltby,' said Dene, as Mrs. Maltby retreated from the room.

'I took the liberty of adding a little thank you present.'

Mr. Budd looked in the bag and took out a large pack of his favourite cigars.

'That's very generous of you, sir. Very generous . . . ' He looked puzzled. 'How did you know . . . ?'

Michael Dene smiled. 'A very simple explanation,' he cut in. 'I just looked up your file.'

Mr. Budd's big face broke into a smile, as he wondered for a few moments just what his file contained . . . Then he asked: 'This Red Fox . . . Kurt Waldburg feller . . . what will happen to 'im?'

'He's to go before a military tribunal. Probably at the Duke of York's, Chelsea — all highly classified. He'll be found guilty of course, and then shot.'

Mr. Budd gave a grunt of satisfaction. He'd watched his bruises change through the colours of the rainbow, and his back still ached.

From outside the room they heard voices and a door closing.

Michael Dene visibly brightened. 'I think one of our chief witnesses has arrived.'

Tania Watts entered looking radiant in a green silk dress.

Michael Dene stepped forward and kissed her on the cheek. 'May I introduce you to Harlequin,' he said to Mr. Budd, with a twinkle in his eye. 'She's one of my best agents.'

Mr. Budd could see by the look in Dene's face, though he tried very hard to conceal it, that he was obviously enamoured with Tania. *Moths to the flame*, he thought. She's done it again! He shook his head slowly with admiration at her sheer audacity.

Dene went over to a tray of glasses and an ice bucket. 'I think we all deserve a glass of Champagne!'

'I'll second that!' said Tania.

GRIM DEATH
MURDER IN MANUSCRIPT
THE GLASS ARROW
THE THIRD KEY
THE ROYAL FLUSH MURDERS
THE SQUEALER
MR. WHIPPLE EXPLAINS
THE SEVEN CLUES
THE CHAINED MAN
THE HOUSE OF THE GOAT
THE FOOTBALL POOL MURDERS
THE HAND OF FEAR
SORCERER'S HOUSE
THE HANGMAN
THE CON MAN
MISTER BIG
THE JOCKEY
THE SILVER HORSESHOE
THE TUDOR GARDEN MYSTERY
THE SHOW MUST GO ON
SINISTER HOUSE
THE WITCHES' MOON
ALIAS THE GHOST

We do hope that you have enjoyed reading this large print book.

Did you know that all of our titles are available for purchase?

We publish a wide range of high quality large print books including:
Romances, Mysteries, Classics
General Fiction
Non Fiction and Westerns

Special interest titles available in large print are:
The Little Oxford Dictionary
Music Book, Song Book
Hymn Book, Service Book

Also available from us courtesy of Oxford University Press:
Young Readers' Dictionary
(large print edition)
Young Readers' Thesaurus
(large print edition)

For further information or a free brochure, please contact us at:
Ulverscroft Large Print Books Ltd.,
The Green, Bradgate Road, Anstey,
Leicester, LE7 7FU, England.
Tel: (00 44) **0116 236 4325**
Fax: (00 44) **0116 234 0205**

A PLAGUE OF SPIES

Michael Kurland

A group of international spies has assembled in the small nation of Alba. Interpol guesses that they aren't there for their holidays — but has no clue as to the real plans being set in motion. Peter Carthage, WAR, Inc.'s slickest agent, is sent to infiltrate and destroy — and ends up captured by an order of most peculiar monks. As Carthage learns the sinister secret of the monastery, he finds himself in the middle of the greatest coup in the history of crime . . .

A MIDWIFE'S CHRISTMAS

Catriona McCuaig

Midwife Maudie and Detective Sergeant Dick Bryant are settling into parenthood, preparing for baby Charlie's first Christmas. But this December will prove to be one of the most eventful in memory. An unknown assailant is attacking multiple Father Christmases. A vulnerable young girl is missing, thrown out by her father in disgrace. And Dick's patience with Maudie's interference in police cases is wearing thin. Meanwhile, there are the politics of the village nativity play to contend with — from protecting soloists' fragile egos to wrangling live farmyard animals. Then a shocking event puts Charlie in danger . . .

THE SILVER CHARIOT KILLER

Richard A. Lupoff

It's Christmas week in New York, and the frozen body of Cletus Berry, Hobart Lindsey's partner, has been found in a back alley alongside that of a known criminal. Was there a connection between the two men? This wouldn't normally be Lindsey's case, but when a man's partner is killed, he must do something about it. Now separated from Marvia Plum, Lindsey is on his own, and the body count is set to rise unless he can solve the mystery of the Silver Chariot . . .

MALICE IN WONDERLAND

Rufus King

Three tales of mystery and the macabre. When the body of a woman clothed in the scantiest of swimsuits is found lying close to the surf on the private beach of a motel, Florida Police Chief Bill Duggan faces a baffling problem. Did she accidentally drown, or commit suicide? Or has she been murdered by one of the very strange guests at the motel? In other stories, a small girl's talent in witchcraft unmasks a killer, and a man's fourth marriage has a fatal ending.

THE RETURN OF THE OTHER MRS. WATSON

Michael Mallory

A new collection of puzzlers featuring the second wife of Dr. John H. Watson, of Sherlock Holmes fame. This time Amelia is plunged into a series of affairs that include the case of a carriage that vanishes into thin air, a jewellery theft on board an ocean liner, and an ancient royal document that may challenge the state of the sovereignty itself. As Amelia solves each case with resourcefulness and wit, she demonstrates the Holmesian adage: 'Once you eliminate the impossible, whatever remains, no matter how improbable, must be the truth.'